TEA IS FOR TAROT

A HAUNTED TEAROOM COZY MYSTERY

KAREN SUE WALKER

LARAGRAY PRESS

ACKNOWLEDGMENTS

My gorgeous cover was designed by Mariah Sinclair, the Cozy Cover Queen. You can find her at https://www.thecovervault.com or on Facebook.

Thank you to Alyssa Lynn Palmer for your copyediting expertise.

It's not easy coming up with new fun recipes, so I'm so grateful to my readers for sending me suggestions. Many, many thanks to Antonia Jennings, Mary Preston, Carol Kurimbokus, and, of course, my very good friend Joan Morrison for providing and/or inspiring the recipes in this book.

Special thanks to my beta readers, typo catchers, and early reviewers—I'm so grateful to you for your support!

Finally, to my wonderful readers. Without you, I wouldn't be having nearly as much fun as I am. Keep on sending me those emails with suggestions, ideas, and pictures of your cats and dogs!

Sign up for email updates at https:// karensuewalker.com and I'll do my best to keep your inbox full of everything cozy.

CHAPTER 1

*O*n a sunny, late-September morning, I drove out of town on a mission. This weekend, my tearoom would host its first psychic fair, and although I'd invited The Amazing Kaslov via email and snail mail, I'd received no response. Maybe he'd accept if I delivered the invitation in person. That was my hope, at any rate.

The road meandered through a dense thicket of fir trees as it climbed up a hill. Just when I thought I must be lost, I maneuvered the car around a sharp turn and gasped at the sight in front of me. The castle stood tall and imposing, much larger than it had appeared when I'd spied it from the top of the lighthouse just outside of town.

Could it really be called a castle when it had been built in the 1980s and not in the medieval period? No lord or lady, earl or baron lived there, just a washed-up magician who'd gone into seclusion decades before.

What else would you call this structure with its grey

stone edifice and turrets? To call it a mansion or a manor house didn't quite do it justice. All it needed was a drawbridge, a moat, and a dungeon to be a full-fledged castle.

A towering wrought-iron gate blocked my way, so I got out of the car and peered through the bars at the imposing structure. I was about to give up and drive home when I spotted a call box next to the gate and pressed the button.

It squawked, and a deep voice came through the speaker. "Who's there?"

"It's April May," I began, wishing I'd rehearsed what to say. "I wonder if I could have a word with Mr. Kaslov."

The voice crackled. "Who are you?"

"April May," I repeated. "I run the SereniTea Tearoom in town. I sent Mr. Kaslov an invitation to participate in our event. It's sort of a psychic, meta-physical fair celebrating all things magical and unknown. I thought—"

"The Amazing Kaslov is not accepting visitors."

"Oh, well, could you—"

"The Amazing Kaslov does not attend amateur events meant to diminish the grandeur and mystery of the illusionist arts. Good day."

"It's nothing like that. I have the utmost respect for the um, illusionist arts." The voice didn't respond. "Could you at least give him my message? Please?"

The intercom fell silent, and I gazed through thick branches and brush, searching for signs of life. Something moved, and I squinted to see who or what had caught my eye.

A petite woman came into view, her long, colorful robe dragging in the grass. Her dark hair, pulled into a chignon, contrasted with her pale face.

I called to her. "Hello?"

She turned her head my way, her blood-red lips in a pout. Indecision or confusion rooted her to the spot until a man's voice called, "Thea!"

Holding one finger up to her lips as if telling me to be quiet, she glided around the side of the house and disappeared from view.

The only sounds were chirping birds and leaves rustling in the soft breeze.

"Weird place," I said to no one. Glancing one more time at the castle, I murmured, "I'd kill to get a look inside."

THE WEEKEND of the Mystics and Magic Fair finally arrived. I'd rearranged the tearoom the night before to get ready for today's event, moving tables around and helping set up displays for our local bookseller and vendors I'd enticed from nearby Somerton. The vendor tables took up one side of the room, while several round tables were spread out to provide a measure of privacy to those having their fortunes told or their cards read.

I fluttered about the room, straightening tablecloths and rearranging chairs. I'd wanted to burn candles, but

Jennifer had convinced me that electric ones would be safer.

My assistant, Jennifer Skillings, who never needed an excuse to dress in costume, emerged from the kitchen wearing a jewel-green Renaissance gown with a brocade corset. "Everything looks perfect."

"Does it?" I gave the room a once-over, not convinced.

"Yes, but your outfit isn't. Don't you want to get changed?"

I sighed and glanced down at my T-shirt and leggings. "I'm waiting until the last minute possible." Jennifer had found a simple, long dress for me to wear. When I'd complained the form-fitting dress left little to the imagination, she'd offered a cape to hide my middle-aged curves. "I'm afraid I'll knock everything over. As soon as I finish up in the kitchen, I'll change."

I pushed the kitchen door open and discovered Irma Vargas, my neighbor and owner of the Mermaid Cafe, sitting at the island munching on the cucumber canapés I'd just prepared. She had a sort of sixth sense that told her when I was making something yummy. Of course, I baked most mornings, so her presence in my kitchen had become routine. I enjoyed her company, not to mention the gossip she often shared.

"Don't eat them all," I scolded. "Those are for the guests."

She frowned. "I'm taste testing them for you. Don't you want to make sure they pass quality control?"

"Good point," I said with a grin. "I feel like royalty with my very own food taster. How kind of you to offer. If any of my food kills you, I'll be sure to give you a nice funeral."

She stuck her tongue out at me then waved toward the front room. "Do you really believe in all this stuff?"

"Stuff?"

"This psychic stuff," she clarified. "Crystal balls and palm reading and all that."

"It's all in fun." I poured each of us a cup of Jasmine tea, calming yet invigorating with its low dose of caffeine. "Although when I first came to town, I laughed at Sarah when she said this house was haunted. I've learned it's best to keep an open mind."

I glanced over at the ghost of Chef Emile Toussaint hunched over the counter scribbling notes in a journal.

"He's here now?" Irma hadn't believed me when I first told her the ghost of the chef she'd once known lived in my kitchen. When I'd told her things only he would know, she eventually came around.

I nodded. "When you start seeing ghosts, it kind of changes your perspective."

"Ghosts?" She raised one eyebrow. "You're seeing more than one now?"

I laughed. "As if one cranky, opinionated French chef isn't enough?" She didn't need to know about all my ghost sightings. "I believe I've sensed Norma a few times. She doesn't like it when you say anything less than flattering about her."

"I've got a few choice words I could say about Norma." She snatched a deviled egg from a tray as I carried it to the refrigerator. "If she hadn't fallen down the stairs when she did, I might have pushed her myself."

The vintage wall clock fell into the sink, and we both jumped. I gave Irma my best "I told you so" glare, but all I got in response was a shrug.

I handed Irma a bowl of roasted chickpeas to keep her busy snacking while I prepared spinach artichoke zucchini bites. I'd been trying to eat more vegetables after my doctor said my regimen of tea sandwiches and quiches was less than ideal.

"I drove over to see The Amazing Kaslov to invite him to our fair, you know," I told Irma.

"You did? What did he say?"

"I didn't get to talk to him. I also mailed him an invitation, though, so you never know."

"Ha! He hasn't left the house in a few decades. Some people think he's dead and they have him propped up in that castle so they can keep collecting his residuals. That TV show of his has been in syndication since it went off the air."

Irma seemed lost in thought as she tapped her fingernails against the side of her teacup. Three fast taps, three slow, then another three fast.

"Are you keeping time to a song in your head?" I asked.

"Huh?" she glanced at her hand. "Funny habit. It's morse code for SOS. Three fast is for the letter 's' and three slow is 'o.'" She grinned and tapped while in a sing-songy voice she said, "Dit-dit-dit, dah-dah-dah, dit-dit-dit. I memorized it as a kid and always thought

6

I'd use it one day to help rescue myself or someone else. Hasn't happened yet."

"You never know," I said. "Especially in this town."

A rap on the back door interrupted us, and Irma stood. "I'll see who that is. You might want to make another batch of those cucumber thingies. They're yummy."

I recognized the voice of Dr. Fredeline Severs, Freddie to her friends, and I could guess who the other voice belonged to. It was soft and lilting with a French accent.

Freddie entered the kitchen and set a cardboard box on the counter before introducing me to her mother. Angeline, tall and slender like her daughter, had dark, luminous skin and hair cut in a short afro.

Freddie opened the box while I asked Angeline about her recent trip to Haiti where she'd been born and raised.

"It's such a long flight," she said. "I only go once or twice a year. It is wonderful to see family and old friends, but also wonderful to return home."

I invited them to take a seat at the island and poured them each a cup of tea while Freddie unpacked the box, handing me several colorful fringed scarves to place over the tablecloths.

"These are beautiful." I touched the delicate fabric. "Are you sure it's okay to use them? What if something gets spilled?"

"I'll never forgive you," Freddie teased. "Just kidding. I found them at a garage sale years ago. I'm glad to finally put them to some use. But here's the *pièce de résistance.*" She set an ornate stand on the island then carefully placed a five- or six-inch crystal ball on it. "I remember this in our house when I was growing up. I used to stare into it for hours, but I never saw anything other than my reflection in it."

I asked Angeline, "Did you bring it from Haiti when you moved here?"

"I bought it at a vintage store when Freddie was just a baby. I used to stare into the glass as well, but I sometimes saw something other than myself."

"I'm so glad you're taking part in our Mystics and Magic Fair. Freddie told me a little about how your mother passed on knowledge to you."

Angeline smiled broadly. "You can say the word, you know."

"What word?"

"Vodou. It's the primary religion of Haiti. I'm a Christian woman, but we have a saying in Haiti that we are seventy percent Catholic, thirty percent Protestant, and a hundred percent Vodou. Haitian Vodou is a spiritual tradition passed down through generations. Since I was raised in Haiti, I grew up with it, and I was surprised at the comments I got from Americans when I moved here for college. We don't stick pins in dolls."

"And telling people's future is part of it?" I asked, my curiosity getting aroused.

She took a sip of her tea. "So many people are suffering. They come to me asking about the future, but what they actually want is hope and guidance. If they ask me about their boyfriend, I tell them they deserve someone who treats them well. I don't have to tell them to stay or go. That's their decision."

"You're like a therapist," I said.

"I am a therapist. I have a master's in social work. Didn't Freddie tell you?"

I shot Freddie a glare. "No. No, she didn't." I threw in a scowl for Irma. "Neither did Irma."

Freddie stifled a snicker. "My mother is a unique woman with many sides to her. I didn't want you to have any preconceived ideas before you met her."

Angeline stood. "We need to go home, Freddie, so I can change. The fair starts in less than an hour."

"I'll bring you back here, but then I have to go into the clinic for a while. I'll see if I can stop by in a few hours."

As soon as Freddie and Angeline left, Irma asked, "Any more deviled eggs?"

I took a plate to the refrigerator for the eggs, adding a couple of cucumber canapés for good measure.

Between bites, Irma said, "On the off chance Kaslov does make an appearance, you'll want to keep him away from Angeline."

"Why is that?"

"Angeline is one of those people who might forgive, but she never forgets."

The sound of the front door opening told me we had a visitor, and I went to see who'd arrived. A middle-aged man wearing a tweed jacket entered through the front door. His green eyes twinkled when I caught his attention.

"Welcome back, Mr. Featherman. Your table looks

ready to go. Your shop has quite a selection of meta-physical and occult books."

"My father was quite the collector. But then, you know that, since you spent some time in the shop before I reopened." He reached into the inside pocket of his jacket and retrieved a small volume, holding it out to me. "I thought you might like this."

I took it and read, "Reading Tea Leaves for Fun and Profit." I opened the leather cover and flipped a few delicate pages. "This looks quite old." It listed several different symbols one might see at the bottom of a teacup.

"Perhaps you can do some fortune-telling of your own," he suggested.

"Maybe I'll give it a try one day when I'm not so busy. I'll let you finish setting up. Thank you for the book."

Stopping by the next table, I said hello to the owner of Mystical Treasures and admired the crystals she had on display, especially a large deep-purple amethyst. I promised myself to stop by later to peruse her jewelry collection and buy a new pair of earrings or perhaps two.

Next to her, a young man who sold candles online set up his table. I'd often ordered from his website, and when I learned he lived not far from Serenity Cove, I invited him to sell at my little fair. He'd also brought incense, and between that and his scented candles, the room was filled with the delightful scent of lavender and vanilla.

I returned to the kitchen just as the buzzer went off.

Jennifer pulled a batch of cheese puffs out of the oven. "Can you even make these faster than Irma can eat them?"

"It's not an easy task," I said with a smirk. "Speaking of Irma, where'd she go?"

"Not sure. But she said she'll be back later."

Irma had left her cup on the island, and I picked it up to carry it to the sink. Looking inside, I imagined what image the tea leaves suggested. One resembled a badger or perhaps a ferret. Another might have been a knife or a sword. I looked up "sword" in the book. It said, "quarrels between lovers or victory of an enemy."

Jennifer watched me. "What are you looking at so intently?"

I showed her the book, and she looked over my shoulder at the cup. "That looks like a castle to me."

"It does?"

She pointed out the turrets and drawbridge, and I finally admitted that she might have a point. I opened to the right page in the book and found the associated meaning: unexpected fortune.

"I'll take mine in tens and twenties," Jennifer said. "Or better yet, a direct deposit into my bank account."

"Sounds good to me." I carried Irma's cup to the sink, taking one more look at the damp leaves inside. It sure looked like a sword to me. Or maybe a ferret with a knife. Tea leaf reading was harder than it seemed.

ANGELINE SOON RETURNED, now wearing a bright red headscarf and an off-the-shoulder blue cotton dress.

"What a lovely outfit," I said. "And those gold hoop earrings pull the whole look together."

"This dress is a traditional Haitian Quadrille. I thought if I were going to tell fortunes, I might as well look the part."

"We'll be starting soon. Shall we join the others and get you settled?" We entered the tearoom, which now resembled an exotic marketplace, with scarf-draped tables, birdcages with colorful paper mâché parrots, and lush ferns I'd rented for the weekend.

Sarah, who ran the Bed and Breakfast in town, sat at a table near the front of the room. Besides Irma, she was the only one who knew that I could see the ghost of Chef Emile Toussaint in my kitchen. She believed in ghosts along with other mysterious phenomena. She also was a chatterbox, but since she nearly always had a positive attitude, I didn't mind.

When she noticed me, she hurried over to show off her outfit. "What do you think?" She wore a long, white-blonde wig and what appeared to be a plus-size Daenerys costume.

"Game of Thrones, right?" I asked to make sure I was on the right page. Her confidence was inspiring, and I wished a little of it would rub off on me. "You look fabulous."

"I do, don't I?" She giggled. "I don't know what this costume has to do with fortune telling, but I hardly ever get a chance to wear it, so I thought, why not?"

"I think it's perfect. This should be fun, don't you think?"

"Oh, yes," she agreed. "I don't know how well I read tarot cards, but I have been practicing. I always like to give an encouraging word to those who might be having a hard time. There have been times in my life when I've felt hopeless, so I know how much of a difference one person's kindness can make."

"I hope those dark times are behind you now," I said. "Permanently."

She grinned. "Oh, yes. I love running the B&B, and I'm so lucky to have a husband who wants all the same things out of life as me. Plus, he doesn't mind listening to me blather on about one thing or another. He may be a quiet man, but you know what they say—still waters run deep."

Before I got depressed about my lack of a life partner, I introduced her to Angeline. They complimented each other on their attire.

"I hope it's okay that I took this table," Sarah said. "Would you prefer it, Angeline? I could sit anywhere. I don't mind at all." She paused, eyeing my outfit. "Is that what you're wearing?"

"Oh!" I'd put off changing as long as I could. "I suppose I'd better get dressed."

I hurried upstairs and slipped into the gown Jennifer had picked out for me, quickly throwing the burgundy velveteen cape over my shoulders. It fell past my knees and had slits to put my hands through, which seemed practical. If it only had pockets too, I might never take it off.

13

As I stepped out into the hallway, I heard Angeline's angry voice and hurried to the landing to see what was happening.

A man stood just inside the door with his sharp chin held high. Strands of limp gray hair stuck out from under his black turban. He flung his cape over one shoulder, revealing red satin lining. It was shorter than mine, but I still felt annoyed that I wasn't the only one in a cape.

"Answer me!" Angeline's voice seethed with anger. "What are you doing here?"

"My dear," the man said, a smug smile on his face. "I was invited."

I scurried down the stairs to greet my new guest. "Welcome. I'm April May."

The man took a deep bow, then took my hand, planting a kiss on the back of it. "My pleasure, Ms. May. I, as you may have guessed, am The Amazing Kaslov."

Ignoring Angeline, who stood nearby with her hands on her hips glaring, I gave a little curtsy. "I'm thrilled you could make it, but I'm afraid I'm not fully prepared for you. The man who spoke to me at your gate implied you don't make appearances."

"There comes a time in one's life when one must face one's demons and return to society, no matter what the risk. The world has been deprived of the insights of The Amazing Kaslov for far too long." Kaslov's voice reminded me of the man who'd spoken to me through the intercom at the castle gate. I'd assumed it had been a servant, but now I felt sure it was Kaslov himself who'd sent me away from the castle. What had made him change his mind about attending my event?

A quick scan of the room and the eyes staring at us told me it might be best to find Kaslov a private space. I knew just the spot. "I've just renovated our study, and I believe it would be the perfect place for you to get settled. If you'd like to join me there, we can discuss how the afternoon will proceed."

He nodded but didn't move. "Is *she* telling fortunes?" He inclined his head in Angeline's direction.

"Um, yes. But..." I wanted to get him away from Angeline. Why was he delaying?

"I would like her to tell my fortune if you don't mind. Unless she lacks the courage to look into the eyes of The Amazing Kaslov and tell him what the future holds."

At these words, Angeline's eyes blazed as if on fire. She grabbed a chair and plopped it in front of her table. "Sit. I will tell you more than you ever wanted to hear."

CHAPTER 2

A hand touched my elbow, and I jumped and turned to face Harriet. I'd first met the round-faced, frizzy-haired woman when she showed up at my tearoom raising funds for the library. To my disappointment, her T-shirt, instead of reading "Fiends of the Library" as it had before, had been replaced by a corrected version.

"Can we talk?" she asked. "Alone?"

"Okay, just give me a sec." I wanted to be present for any fireworks between Kaslov and Angeline.

Kaslov took the seat across from Angeline. She pulled her crystal ball closer and gazed into the glass while he smirked. I wanted to smack him across the head for treating Angeline so disrespectfully.

"Now?" Harriet said, an urgent tone in her voice.

Reluctantly, I led Harriet to the kitchen. When I swung the door open, Chef Emile looked up, narrowing his eyes in annoyance. I took a seat at the island and gestured toward one of the other stools, but Harriet paced instead.

"I've always thought very highly of you," she began, walking to the sink and back again.

"That's nice." She'd never given me the slightest impression that she admired me, but I waited for her to tell me what was on her mind.

She stopped pacing, folded her arms over her chest, and said, "I'm concerned about you."

"Huh?" That came out of left field. "Why would you be concerned?"

"This fascination you have with the dark arts."

I burst into laughter. "The dark arts?"

Harriet scowled. "It's not funny at all. There are even rumors that you're seeing ghosts. You are dabbling in things you don't understand, April. Next thing you know, you'll be practicing witchcraft and devil worship."

I took a deep breath, fighting my impulse to tell her she was crazy. "It's all in fun, Harriet. I'm convinced there's magic in the world, but I don't believe in evil spirits or witches. I believe, above all, in the goodness of people."

"Not everyone is good, you know. Some are evil. We've had murders here in our very own town."

"I know that as well as anyone." Better than anyone since I'd helped put a couple of the killers behind bars. "I'll still keep believing in good people. And I promise I won't take up devil worship in my spare time." Perhaps I sounded too flippant with my last comment because it didn't seem to appease her.

"But what is that man doing here?" she asked.

"The Amazing Kaslov?"

She scowled and shook her head slowly as if delivering bad news. "He's the devil."

"Excuse me?"

"Not *the* devil, the one who lives down there." She pointed at the floor. "But Kaslov is a terrible person. Don't tell me you don't know what he did." With a snort, she stormed off.

I watched the door swing back and forth until it came to a stop. "What don't I know about Kaslov?" I muttered. "And why hasn't anyone told me?" I turned to Chef Emile who appeared busy writing. "Do you know anything?"

Chef looked up as if he hadn't been listening to every word. "I know many things. For one, I know I prefer peace and quiet, and I suspect I shall get little of either for the remainder of the day."

"Do me a favor, would you?" I asked. "Keep your eyes and ears open. I'll check back with you later."

I didn't know that ghosts could roll their eyes, but Chef Emile did it as well as any teenage girl.

Hoping to overhear Angeline and Kaslov as she told his fortune, I picked up a tray of open-faced radish sandwiches to take into the tearoom. As I entered the room, Harriet walked out the front, letting the screen door slam behind her. Perhaps it was best that she left early.

Meanwhile, everyone else in attendance pretended not to listen to Angeline's every word.

"I see a woman," Angeline said, her eyes focused on

the crystal ball before her. "She could have had a long and happy life if not for your actions."

Kaslov shrugged. "There have been many women in my life. Perhaps you can be more specific?"

The tension in the room grew as Angeline's eyes narrowed in repressed anger. As she continued gazing into the glass, her expression changed into confusion.

"The woman believes she is in love with you." She paused and glanced up at Kaslov before adding softly, "A young woman."

Kaslov didn't attempt to hide his smirk. "I have many female fans, some of them young and rather persistent. It is one of the hazards of fame."

Angeline closed her eyes tightly, and I imagined her reciting a calming affirmation to herself. It didn't seem to work.

Angeline opened her eyes and stared at Kaslov. "You will get what's coming to you." She must not have gotten the reaction she wanted, because she added, "Death is in your future."

No one spoke for what felt like several seconds and then Kaslov began to laugh.

He stood and addressed the room. "Perhaps you haven't heard, but sad to say, death is in all of our futures. I have built my career and my legacy on rather more profound prognostications."

Several people hurried over to Kaslov to speak with him. Angeline came up to me and grabbed my arm, leading me to the kitchen.

As soon as the door closed behind us, Angeline spoke through clenched teeth. "That man!"

I poured her a cup of my favorite rose petal black tea in hopes it might calm her.

She took in a sharp breath, then let it out slowly. Very slowly. "Why do I let him get to me? I know better." She took the teacup from me, held it up to her face, and breathed in the fragrant steam. She closed her eyes, but her clenched jaw betrayed her emotions.

"You're only human, apparently," I reassured her. "Like the rest of us."

That brought a hint of a smile to her face. She nodded toward the tearoom. "You have an event going on. You'd better get back out there." When I didn't move, she added, "I'll be fine."

Not wanting to leave her alone in such a state, I poked my head into the tearoom. A man I didn't recognize stood talking with Mr. Featherman at his book display. Jennifer fussed over the buffet table, arranging trays, and neatly lining up plates and napkins.

In the corner, Harriet sat stuffing cucumber canapes into her mouth. When had she returned? She stared at something or someone, and when I followed her gaze, I saw who held her attention.

The Amazing Kaslov leaned over Sarah's shoulder, whispering in her ear as she softly giggled. The front door opened, and a thin, nondescript man entered. His survey of the room stopped when he spotted Sarah and Kaslov. Something about him seemed familiar. He didn't appear happy to see Kaslov flirting so openly and Sarah appearing to enjoy it.

The moment I recognized the altogether forgettable

man was Sarah's husband, I called out, "Hello! Nice to see you again."

"Uh-huh," he replied.

I glanced over my shoulder at Sarah who went pale before she plastered a smile on her face and hurried over to us.

"Simon," she said, taking his arm. "I didn't think you were coming. Was Fran able to cover the front desk after all?"

"Uh-huh."

His one-word answers began to unsettle me. Wanting to smooth over the awkward moment, I suggested Sarah show him around. "Help yourselves to the buffet, especially you, Sarah. You'll probably be busy doing readings most of the afternoon, so this might be your only chance to get a bite to eat."

Before someone else got The Amazing Kaslov's attention, I wanted a word with him. I approached him and asked, "Can we talk for a minute? I'll show you the study and we can go over some details."

He followed me into the study where I'd hung drapes over the doorway. I held back the velveteen fabric and motioned for Kaslov to enter, waiting for his reaction. The room had been completely redone in the style of an old English manor library with dark wood paneling, tall bookcases, and brocade upholstery.

My handyman, Mark, had done an amazing job on the room but he didn't stick around to see the final touches I made with the furniture and drapes. After his unfortunate love affair ended in betrayal and tragedy, he went on an extended vacation. Standing in this room made me miss him.

Kaslov examined a small pedestal table I'd arranged in the center of the room with Queen Anne chairs on either side. "This will do."

Hiding my disappointment at his lukewarm reaction to my décor and Mark's skilled workmanship, I gestured for him to take a seat on the far side of the table, and I sat across from him.

While I explained my system to charge for readings, with each $20 ticket good for a fifteen-minute session, two tickets for half an hour, and so forth, he stifled a yawn. I added that all proceeds were earmarked for the Save the Otters foundation. "They're endangered, you know."

When I finished speaking, he said, "I will accept cash only. You may do what you wish with your other so-called psychics."

I felt my shoulders tighten with irritation. "This event is a fundraiser, Mr. Kaslov. I'm donating the food and providing my tearoom, my time, and my assistant's time. The others are donating their services so that all the proceeds can go directly to the charity."

"Your other so-called fortune tellers are amateurs. The Amazing Kaslov will bring more people to your little fair. That is my contribution."

I felt my irritation grow. "That might have been true if you'd RSVP'd for the event. I would have been able to publicize your appearance, and we might have gotten more visitors as a result. As it is, no one even knows you're here."

"Be that as it may, I will accept only cash. Fifty dollars for a half-hour session. At the end of the day, I will provide my own donation to your seal charity as I see fit."

"Otters." My jaw clenched, and I knew I had to choose between making a scene by kicking him out or accepting his conditions.

"Fine." I stood to go. "It had better be a good donation, or..." I wasn't sure how I wanted to end the sentence.

"Or, what, my dear?" A thin smile did nothing to hide his arrogant expression.

"Or I won't invite you back." It was a meaningless threat, but I knew better than to say what I wanted to. I stood. "I'll leave you to get settled."

"Very well," he said, not bothering to get up. "I will be ready for my first client in ten minutes."

Returning to the tearoom, I found several visitors milling about. Mr. Featherman chatted with two young women. One of them, casually dressed in jeans and a zip-up sweatshirt, had long, dark hair that fell over her shoulders in soft waves. She appeared quite interested in one of his books, and they carried on an animated conversation.

"Do you have anything by Jilly Myers?" the other, a blonde in a knee-length dress asked. "I heard she had a new book come out."

Thinking I'd met the dark-haired woman before, I strolled over to say hello, but Harriet blocked my way.

She held up a ticket. "I want to see The Amazing Kaslov."

"You do?" I asked, perplexed. "I thought you said he was evil."

She stared at the floor and mumbled, "I'm willing to be flexible."

"Is that so?" Not sure what to make of her about-face, I took her statement at face value. "I'm sorry to tell you he's only accepting cash. Fifty dollars for a half-hour of his time. I'm starting to think you might be right about him. He's not a nice man."

She frowned, and the lines between her brows deepened. "Fifty dollars?"

"Yep. I'd get your fortune told by Angeline or Sarah if I were you."

Harriet hesitated, appearing uncertain about what to do. She fished in her purse and pulled out her wallet, counting the bills inside. "Okay," she announced. "I've got enough."

"Really?" I glanced at the clock. "Wait five minutes and go on in." I wasn't going to bother announcing people like I was his personal assistant.

Jennifer stood by the front door greeting guests and selling tickets for readings. I told her what The Amazing Kaslov had said.

Jennifer shrugged. "I'd never heard of the guy before today, but if people want to throw away their money, that's their business. I'm not going to encourage anyone to see him if he's not helping raise money for the otters."

"We'll see what he contributes when we're done." I surveyed the room until my eyes came to rest on the buffet table. "Boy, these people can eat. Would you mind refreshing the appetizers? I'll cover the door for a while."

"Gladly."

Jennifer hurried off, happy for something to do. At her age, I was full of energy too, but now I liked nothing better than a comfortable chair.

I chatted with neighbors who wandered in out of curiosity and others who were fans of new-age ideas and esoteric philosophies. One couple, wearing matching tie-dyed T-shirts, drove all the way from San Francisco. I glanced at the curtained door behind which Harriet and Kaslov were meeting, wishing I could be a fly on the wall. Did Harriet spend fifty dollars for an audience with Kaslov just to tell him off?

Jennifer scurried over to tell me everyone seemed to enjoy the buffet and it needed refilling again. "Should I put some hot appetizers into the oven?"

"I'll take care of that if you'll watch the door again." When I saw her look of disappointment, I added, "Just for a few minutes."

I headed for the kitchen to bake more cheese puffs and polenta bites. As I passed the study, the curtain swept open, and Harriet emerged, her face red and blotchy. She rushed past me, slipping through the kitchen door. I followed her to see if she needed sympathy, a nice cup of tea, or both.

As I pushed the kitchen door open, someone from outside shouted, "Fire!" The voice came from the side of the house where my car sat parked in the driveway.

I dashed into the kitchen, grabbed the fire extinguisher, and ran out the back door joining ten or so others gathered in the driveway. Smoke billowed from one of the trash cans lined up next to the house.

"Step aside," I called out. Having read the instructions several times in anticipation of an emergency, I quickly put out the fire. The bystanders cheered, and I took a little bow.

My neighbor, a dowdy woman who hadn't said a kind word to me since I moved in, called over her fence where she'd been watching the whole time. "You should be more careful. You're lucky your house didn't burn down."

I ignored her and returned to the fair, where Mr. Featherman and the other vendors had remained dutifully by their tables. I let them know the crisis had been averted.

Jennifer pointed out the appetizer trays on the buffet table were nearly empty.

"I've got appetizers ready to go in the oven. They'll be ready in fifteen minutes, as long as we don't have another crisis."

"Anyone else request a meeting with The Amazing Kaslov?" she asked, sarcastically emphasizing the word "amazing."

"Not a one," I admitted. "I'm peeved that he's such a scrooge. I mean, who doesn't love otters?"

In the kitchen, I retrieved two trays of uncooked appetizers from the refrigerator. Before I could put them in the oven, I heard a woman scream. Bursting from the kitchen, I almost ran right into Jennifer.

She pointed at the study. "The scream came from there."

I pushed the curtain aside and stepped into the study. Sarah stood in the middle of the room, with her hands pressed to her cheeks. On the floor, The Amazing Kaslov lay face down, a knife in his back.

While I waited for Deputy Molina, our one-man police force, to arrive, I visually inspected the room. It felt eerie being in a room with a dead body, but I knew by experience that once Molina arrived, I'd be shut out of the investigation. This might be my only chance to search for clues.

Taking care not to touch anything or move further into the room and take the chance of stepping on evidence, I took inventory. One teacup and saucer on the table. Two chairs, one on its side, possibly indicating a struggle. His cape lay on the floor.

A man is dead. Of course, there was a struggle.

"But he was stabbed in the back," I muttered. "If you're fighting with someone, how do you stab them in the back? Maybe knock them down first?"

Kaslov's face didn't appear red or bruised, or at least not the side of his face I could see. Someone would have to be strong to knock down a full-sized man, which might rule out a woman unless she was a weightlifter. Or an older man, like Mr. Featherman. Although he wasn't much older than me, come to think about it, and he might be stronger than he looked.

We'd all know more after Freddie had examined the body. I sucked in a breath when I spotted the gold hoop earring next to Kaslov's cape. The curtain swung open behind me.

I greeted our thirty-something, baby-faced, acting police chief. "Hello, Deputy Molina."

"What are you doing in here?" he asked, practically growling.

"Just keeping an eye on things. Not touching anything." I held up my hands to emphasize the point. "Not even moving."

"Well, you can move now. Go out into the main room with the others. A junior deputy will arrive shortly from the county sheriff's office to help keep order."

"Let me know if you need anything." He didn't say anything, so I suggested, "A cup of tea, perhaps?"

"You discovered the body?"

"No, that was Sarah. I heard her scream and—"

"Send her in so I can have a word with her."

"In here? Wouldn't that risk contaminating the crime scene?" I tried not to sound like a know-it-all, but sometimes I can't help it.

"I'll meet her at the doorway," he snarled.

The moment I emerged from the room, all I wanted to do was talk with Angeline, but following Molina's orders, I first went looking for Sarah.

When I found Sarah, I informed her that Deputy Molina wanted a word with her. "He'll meet you at the study door."

"Where the dead body is?" she asked, voice quivering. When I nodded, she plodded toward the curtains, arriving at the doorway just as Molina stepped out.

Several people surrounded me, peppering me with questions. I answered the most pressing one first. "Yes, the Amazing Kaslov is dead," followed by, "I can't give you any details." Every answer after that was a version of, "I don't know," and, "We'll have to wait to see what the deputy has to say."

Sarah returned to my side and grabbed hold of my arm just as Dr. Fredeline Severs arrived. I wanted to pull Freddie aside to tell her about the earring I'd found that looked exactly like one her mother had been wearing, but she passed by and disappeared through the curtains. Telling Sarah I'd be right back, I followed Freddie into the study and stood just inside the doorway, ignoring the glare Molina gave me.

Freddie walked straight to the body and stood looking down on it. "Who is this?"

"The Amazing Kaslov," I said.

Freddie gave me an odd look. "No, it isn't."

CHAPTER 3

*M*olina kicked me out of the study before I could ask any questions. If the man who'd arrived in my house that afternoon in a cape and turban wasn't The Amazing Kaslov, then who the heck was he?

Harriet came up to me. "The officer said not to leave, but I have to get to the library and open the bookstore. I'm the only one scheduled to volunteer today."

It occurred to me that Molina would want to ask Harriet why she'd been so angry after her meeting with Kaslov, but I kept that to myself for now. "A deputy from the sheriff's office should be arriving soon. I'm sure as soon as he gets your information, he'll allow you to leave."

Moments later, the other deputy arrived, and I greeted him with Harriet close behind me.

"I need to leave," Harriet said. "You can't keep me here." She tried to step around him to get to the door.

The young man held up his hand to stop her. "I need to speak with Deputy Molina and get instructions before anyone can leave."

As I passed by the study, Molina emerged and asked to speak with Angeline.

"I'll go get her." I wanted to talk with her first, but he followed close behind me on my way to the kitchen. Hoping to get rid of him for a few minutes, I gestured toward the front door. "Your deputy is waiting for instructions."

Molina called out to the young man. "I'll be right there."

Angeline greeted us from the kitchen island where she sipped a cup of tea. My heart sank at the sight of her naked ears, and I crossed my fingers that both of her earrings were safely in her pocket.

With a smile, she said, "I hope you don't mind me helping myself to a cup of tea, April. What an awful thing to happen. I never liked the man, but I never would have wished him dead."

Her expression didn't agree with her words. What had he done to make her hate him so much?

"Well, actually, as it turns out..." I began.

Molina held up a hand, stopping me from telling her the dead man was not The Amazing Kaslov after all. He returned his attention to Angeline. "I'd like a word with you, in private, if I may."

Angeline nodded. "Of course, deputy. I'm not sure that I can tell you anything that will help you, but I'm happy to answer your questions."

Deputy Molina glared at me, which I took as a

signal that he wanted me to leave. He followed me to the kitchen door. "Anything you have learned that is not general knowledge is to stay that way, do you understand?" He lowered his voice to a whisper. "Especially the identity of the victim."

"But I don't even know who the victim is, deputy."

"You know who he isn't," he said. "Keep that information to yourself for the time being."

I turned back to Angeline, hoping to catch her eye. She smiled, and I tugged at my ear, but she didn't catch on.

Chef held a wooden spoon and a bowl, and I wondered what he was making before remembering it wasn't real. He looked up and I cupped my hand around my ear to signal I wanted him to listen to Molina's and Angeline's conversation. He gave me a bored sigh and went back to his preparations.

Pushing open the door into the front room I looked around. A few visitors remained, speaking in hushed voices, probably sharing rumors about the murder.

If I couldn't talk to Angeline, Freddie would be my second choice. The earring would be incriminating evidence, and Angeline gave herself a good motive when she'd berated him in front of everyone. I was about to go to the study door and ask to speak with Freddie when Molina emerged from the kitchen and strode straight over to me.

"You're next," he said. "Wait for me in the kitchen while I talk to my deputy."

Time alone with Chef Emile was just what I'd hoped for. I pushed through the door, fingers crossed my ghost had paid attention during Angeline's interview.

Wasting no time, I asked Chef, "What did you hear?"

He stirred the mixture in the bowl. "It was quite uninteresting. Why do you care?"

"Angeline might be a murder suspect. I need to make sure she doesn't end up in jail." When he didn't respond, I figured I'd try a direct question. "Did he ask her about her earring?"

Chef raised an eyebrow. "He did not mention jewelry."

"No?" That seemed odd. "Did he ask her about what she and Kas—" I reminded myself that the dead man was not The Amazing Kaslov. "Did he ask about what she and the victim talked about in the study?"

"Ah, yes. I believe he did."

"And?" I prompted, getting impatient. Molina might return any moment. "What did she say?"

"The woman, her name is Angeline, you say?" When I nodded impatiently, he continued. "She said she did not enter the study this afternoon."

"She said that?"

The door swung open, and Molina entered. "Who are you talking to?"

"Just myself. I do it all the time. Jennifer's always teasing me about it."

Molina and I had been through this before. He would take notes while I described the events of the day.

But first I had questions. "How did no one recognize that this man wasn't Kaslov? Not Angeline or any of the neighbors?"

"I asked Ms. Severs just that question," Molina said. "She claimed she hadn't seen Kaslov in thirty years. So, when this guy showed up around the same age and build, she didn't question if it was him."

"He had the accent down." I recalled the haughty tone and the way he enunciated certain words. But then he had hours of video from Kaslov's TV show he could use to practice and perfect his impersonation.

Molina asked me to start from the beginning when the man first arrived earlier that day. When I got to the part about the fire, he stopped me.

"Tell me everyone who you saw outside at that time," he ordered, flipping his notebook to a new page.

"Was that when the murder happened?" I asked.

He grunted with annoyance. "Just answer the question."

After giving it some thought, I listed everyone I remembered seeing in the driveway while I put out the fire, including Jennifer. I described several people whose names I didn't know as best as I could.

"Not Angeline?" he asked.

"I didn't see her out there, but I might not have noticed. I was kind of busy putting out a fire. I also didn't see any of the vendors. Mr. Featherman stayed inside, and I think the others did too."

"That's good information. Hopefully, they saw something."

I nodded, also hopeful. "Unfortunately, you can't see the study door from where the tables were set up."

With all the commotion, I doubted they would have paid attention to everyone's comings and goings. The fire was a convenient distraction for the murderer. Or perhaps... "Do you think the murderer set the fire so he wouldn't be noticed going in and out of the study?"

Molina cleared his throat, a sure sign I was getting on his nerves. "What happened when you came back inside?"

"The buffet looked pretty empty, so I went into the kitchen to heat up some more appetizers. That's when I heard Sarah scream and I ran into the study."

"Tell me what you found when you entered the room."

I decided to take him literally and only tell him what I noticed when I first entered. I described Sarah standing next to the body of the person we all thought was The Amazing Kaslov. "Have you figured out who he really is?"

He narrowed his eyes. "That will be all for now."

Neither of us moved for a moment, and I wondered if he intended to use my kitchen for all his interviews.

Not wanting to be kicked out from the source of food and drink, and being in need of a strong cup of tea, I proactively asked, "Would you like to use one of the upstairs rooms for your remaining interviews?"

He took the hint and stood. "I believe you have an upstairs parlor. I think I can find it myself."

When Chef and I were alone again, I asked, "Did you see anyone come in here when the fire started outside?"

"What fire?" he asked.

"You didn't notice people yelling and running around an hour or so ago?" He might be dead, but I thought he saw and heard everything that went on in the vicinity of the kitchen.

"Oh that," he said in a bored voice. "You cannot expect me to pay attention to every little thing that happens in your world."

~

MOLINA QUESTIONED the vendors while the young deputy took brief statements and collected contact information for the remaining guests. I bought a few candles and a pair of earrings, feeling somehow responsible for the lack of sales due to the event ending early. Mr. Featherman returned from his interview with Molina and began packing up his books.

He gave me some encouraging words. "You can't control what happens to you. You can only control your reaction."

"Very wise words."

He chuckled softly. "Not always easy advice to follow." He tucked a small box of books under his arm and reached out to shake my hand. "Don't let this failure keep you from trying new things. And don't be a stranger. Stop by and check out the bookstore when you can. I've made some changes."

"I'll do that." As he turned to go, I stopped him. "When the fire happened, did you see anything in here?"

He gave me an indulgent smile. "The deputy asked me not to share what I told him with anyone."

"Did he happen to mention me by name when he said that?"

His smile broadened, but he didn't answer, which was enough of a response for me. Still, my concern for Freddie's mother made me ask one more question. "So, you can't tell me if you saw Angeline indoors when most of us were outside."

He shook his head. "Sometimes it's better not to ask questions when you're not going to like the answer."

As he walked away, I asked myself what he meant. Surely, he didn't think Angeline was a murderer. Or did he?

Nearly an hour later, after the last two guests gave the young officer their contact information, I walked them to the door and thanked them for coming.

"I wouldn't want to be in Angeline's shoes after what she said to him," one of the women said.

"I'm pretty sure everyone heard," the other added. "The detective must know all about it by now."

I closed the door behind them and walked through the now-empty room. Yellow tape stretched across the study door. The mystery man's body had been removed, but Freddie and Deputy Molina stayed behind. Freddie would be doing her forensics thing while Molina searched for additional clues, I supposed, and dusted for fingerprints.

Somewhere I had the card of a company that did crime scene clean up—probably in the junk drawer. I hadn't expected to need it again, but I wasn't good at getting rid of things, even business cards.

I found Angeline with Jennifer at the kitchen island having a cup of tea, a half-full plate of appetizers in front of them. Emile gave me a quick look, then pretended to be occupied stirring a pot on the stove. "Oh, you're still here, Angeline."

"My ride is busy with her coroner duties," Angeline said. "She should be done soon."

"I offered Angeline a ride home, but she wanted to wait for Freddie," Jennifer said. "Sit down and have something to eat. I bet you haven't had a bite all day, have you?"

My stomach grumbled, reminding me she was right. "You've been on your feet all day too. I'll get it." I poured myself a cup of tea and grabbed a plate from the cupboard. As I was about to sit down, loud voices came from the other part of the house. I pushed the kitchen door open a few inches. "Do you hear that?" Molina must have finished his interviews and rejoined Freddie in the study.

"What are they arguing about?" Jennifer asked.

I leaned my head out, hoping to catch their words. "I'm not sure, but I've never heard Freddie sound that angry." I let the door swing closed and took a seat at the island.

"I have," Angeline said with a smirk. "That girl has a strong personality. She doesn't let anyone push her around, let me tell you."

I had a feeling I knew what Molina and Freddie were fighting about. "Angeline, where are those beautiful hoop earrings you were wearing earlier?" I did my best to make the question sound casual. "They complimented your outfit so nicely."

Angeline's hand went to her ear. "I dropped one somewhere, so I took the other one off. I haven't been able to find it anywhere. Would you keep an eye out for it when you clean up? They're one of my favorite pairs."

"I'm sure we'll find it around here somewhere," I said, not wanting to say more in front of Jennifer.

She stood. "In fact, why don't I help you clean. It will give me something to do while I wait."

Before I could respond to her offer, Freddie burst into the room. Without a glance to Jennifer or me, she announced to her mother, "We're leaving."

"What's going on?" I asked.

Freddie shook her head. "Not now." She and her mother quickly gathered up their things and hurried out the back door. The moment they left, Deputy Molina entered.

He perused the room, taking stock of the surroundings, his eyes finally coming to rest on me. "I would like another word with you, Ms. May."

Jennifer stood and asked the deputy if he had any additional questions for her.

He thought for a moment. "If I do, I'll get in touch."

She turned to me. "My grandmother is making dinner for my dad and me."

"How nice." Jennifer's grandmother Helen who she'd met for the first time a few weeks earlier, had rented a cottage in town, and Jennifer spent much of her free time with her. As a side bonus to Helen's reappearance, Jennifer and her father seemed to be healing their relationship. After all the heartache the father and daughter had experienced, they deserved some peace and happiness.

I set out more appetizers for Molina and me. We had plenty of leftover food since the event had been cut short.

"Help yourself, deputy." I handed him a plate and napkin, then poured him a cup of tea. It had gone lukewarm, but I had a feeling he wouldn't mind.

"Thank you." He took a seat, and his shoulders relaxed as he gulped his tea. "It's been quite a day."

"To say the least." As impatient as I was to learn the identity of the man who'd impersonated Kaslov, I held off asking. Perhaps if I shared what I knew, the deputy might do the same. "I've been giving it some thought, and I'm pretty sure that the man in the study is the same person I talked to through the intercom at The Amazing Kaslov's home. His voice and his manner of speaking were similar."

He stopped as he was about to take another sip of tea. "Is that so? I've left several messages for Victor Kaslov, but he hasn't returned my calls. I had a feeling the victim might be connected to him in some way, and you've just confirmed it. You think he worked for him?"

I nodded. "Do you think whoever killed the fake Kaslov meant to kill the real one?"

He shrugged, stuffing a canapé in his mouth. It wouldn't be easy getting information out of him, but then it never was. By now he should realize I was an ally he could trust. I'd think he'd value my opinion after all we'd been through together in the short time he'd been acting Police Chief for Serenity Cove.

"Were you able to I.D. him from his fingerprints?" I asked.

He washed down his last bite with a gulp of tea before answering. "I was."

I sighed in frustration. "You know I'm going to find out sooner or later."

"Fine." He pressed his lips into a hard line. "But it goes no further than this room. His name was Orson Jennings. Not a lot on his rap sheet, but he'd had a few brushes with the law. Nothing recent. No current address listed."

"You think he's using an alias?" I asked.

"Might be. Some people don't like hiring a thief."

"A thief?" Now that was interesting information.

He wiped his mouth with a napkin and stood. "I'm going to see Kaslov now. Let me know if you think of any additional information you forgot to mention." He emphasized the word "forgot" as if I might be holding information from him.

If he was as good of a detective as he seemed to think he was, he already knew that the earring found in the study belonged to Angeline. I wasn't going to be the one to tell him.

CHAPTER 4

$\mathcal{I}$ stared into my cup. The tea had gone cold, but I didn't have the energy to make a fresh pot. It would taste great iced, but I was even too tired to walk to the freezer for ice cubes. Why had Orson Jennings come to my event? And why had he chosen to impersonate The Amazing Kaslov?

He must have done it for money. No other reason made sense. He might have walked away with a few hundred dollars if he hadn't been killed first.

That reason didn't make sense to me either. He had a job, after all, which he might have lost if he'd been found out. What little I knew of Kaslov led me to believe he'd be furious.

Maybe it was the excitement of pretending to be a famous man who commanded so much respect and admiration. He also inspired hatred, but maybe Orson didn't know about Kaslov's enemies.

Emile interrupted my thoughts. "The woman who was here earlier. Why does she speak with a French accent? Is she from France?" He poured the contents of the saucepan into a bowl.

"She's from Haiti. It was once a French colony known as St. Dominique. After a revolution, it became only the second independent country in the Western Hemisphere. The United States was the first, of course."

"And they still speak French?" he asked.

"My understanding is that their version of the language is quite close to what is spoken in France. Angeline grew up there until she went off to college. She met Dr. Severs, Freddie's father, and they settled here in Serenity Cove."

"It is a long time since I've heard the language spoken." Emile gave a small sigh and turned away.

I'd wanted to ask him if Angeline had said anything pertinent to the murder, but he appeared lost in thought. I supposed it was lonely being a ghost with only one person to keep you company. Lucky for him, he got me as his one mortal companion. He had no idea what boring lives so many people lived.

IT HAD BEEN months since I'd taken a Sunday off. Jennifer invited me to join her at her church, but I wanted some alone time. I hoped that God could hear my prayers just as well from my home, although he didn't always give me what I asked for. I supposed He had different priorities than me.

Sitting with my coffee and my thoughts, the sound

of the back door startled me. "Must be Irma," I mumbled. She would know I had leftovers from the event.

Instead, Angeline stepped into the kitchen, dressed casually yet elegantly. She could probably make sweats look stylish. I offered her a cup of coffee.

"I brought back Sarah's tarot cards." She took a seat at the island, pulling a pack from her purse and placing it in front of her. "I forgot all about them."

I picked up the box. "Medieval Cat tarot?"

She chuckled. "I was surprised too. But you should check out the cards. The illustrations are quite lovely."

I placed them in front of her. "Why don't you tell my fortune?"

"Very well." She opened the deck and shuffled the cards, then asked me to cut them. "Now, hold them in your hands and silently ask the question you want answered."

I held the cards, my mind swimming with all the questions I wanted answered, like, *Why are you really here, Angeline?* I finally settled on just one and handed her back the deck.

"In Haiti, regular playing cards are used to foresee the future, just as they once were in other parts of the world," she explained as she laid out four cards face down clockwise, placing a fifth card in the center. "But it's not about the cards, really. It's about connecting with your intuition."

"I see."

She turned over the first card that she'd placed at the top, which displayed a cat figure in a dress with wings pouring water into a jug. "Temperance. These cards can be read much like you might tell a story. The first card is the foundation of the answer—what is known in the present."

"Temperance? As in avoiding alcohol?"

"This card is about balance. True balance is never achieved in the moment, but in the ebb and flow of life, one can find peace. This card may be telling us that the balance of your world has been upended and you seek to restore it."

"I see. Pretty accurate considering what happened here yesterday."

"That's very true." She flipped the card to her right. "Four of cups. Interesting."

"Why do you say that?" I asked.

"The position of this card indicates past obstacles. You see how the man, or rather," she chuckled softly, "in this case the cat, is ignoring the cup offered to them?" When I nodded, she explained, "You may have been so involved in your own emotions or situation that you ignored the help you were offered."

"It's more like other people ignore it when I try to help," I groused. Like Deputy Molina.

She raised her eyebrows and smiled sweetly as if indulging me. Touching the card closest to her, she said, "This card represents hidden influences." She flipped it over. "Six of coins. You see how the cat is giving coins away? This might mean that you will provide much-needed assistance, but based on the location of the card, your role won't be out in the open."

"That sounds par for the course." Maybe Molina would let me help with the investigation if I kept quiet about it.

I watched as she turned over the card on the left. "The Devil." Harriet had called Kaslov the devil. "Does this represent Satan or just general run-of-the-mill evil?" I asked. The cat-person pictured on the card wore a plumed hat and stood among flames.

"The cards are not literal, which is why they must be interpreted by someone with an understanding of the deeper meanings they hold. Whether one believes in the devil or not, we are all familiar with evil." She picked up the card for a closer look. "That's unusual." She held the card out to me. "The cat is wearing a mask. We all wear masks in life, some to hide behind and some to stay safe from judgment."

"And some to hide evil?"

She nodded and turned over the center card. "The Tower." A look of concern passed over her features which she quickly shook off, giving me a smile. "Even in times of disaster, there is always divine intervention."

"Disaster?" I didn't like the sound of that.

She laughed, but it sounded forced. "The cards can be quite dramatic at times." She stood and threw her purse over her shoulder.

"So can life." I decided to ask my other question. "Why did you really come here this morning? You could have dropped the cards off at Sarah's Bed and Breakfast."

She blinked. "Oh, that. I almost forgot. I wanted to

see if you'd found my other earring. That pair is one of my favorites."

"You don't know?" I asked, and she gave me a questioning look in return. Wouldn't Freddie have told her? Molina had been very stern advising me not to share information. "You should ask your daughter."

"She has it?" Without waiting for an answer, she added, "That's good to hear."

I glanced at Chef, wondering if he could tell somehow if Angeline was lying or not.

She followed my gaze. "What is it? What are you looking at?"

"Nothing," I said innocently.

She became still and silent staring in Chef's direction. For a moment, I almost thought she could see him.

"*Que fait-elle?*" he asked. "What is she doing? Have you told this woman also about me?"

Her eyes widened. "*Je vous sens. Êtes-vous bon ou mauvais?*"

"*Bien sûr que non,*" Chef replied. "*Je suis un simple cuisiner.*"

"Zut alors," I said. When her head jerked toward me, I gave her a shrug. "That's the only French I know other than 'please' and 'thank you.'"

"The spirit speaks to you," she said, her voice curious. "How is this? Does my daughter know about your gift?"

There seemed little point in denying it. "Your daughter is a doctor. I'm pretty sure she doesn't believe in things like ghosts."

She smiled and shrugged. "You're right. She doesn't."

"If you want to hear about my spirit as you call him, you might as well get comfortable." I put the kettle on and searched through the cupboard. When I found the oolong tea, I scooped it into the infuser. While waiting for the water to boil, I began to tell her about Chef Emile Toussaint, starting with the first time I'd seen him standing in the kitchen of my new home.

While I talked, Angeline sipped her tea, listening intently. Chef watched the two of us carefully and interrupted me whenever he disagreed with my version of events.

Angeline occasionally asked questions. "And you don't know why he never leaves this room?"

"No. And if he knows the reason, he's not telling me."

"I see." She paused, as if hesitant to say something. "Would you ask him…if he's happy?" she began.

"You can ask him yourself. He can hear you just fine." I grinned. "I think he would like to hear you speak French."

She mirrored my smile and turned in his direction. "*Monsieur le chef. Êtes-vous heureux?*"

Chef's expression was unreadable, almost as if he didn't understand the question. He sighed. "*Je cuisine toute la journée, mais je ne sens rien.*"

I asked him to say it again more slowly and repeated it to Angeline. "What does it mean?"

She translated. "He cooks all day, and he cannot taste a thing."

"How sad." I hadn't ever thought how frustrating it must be when the one thing you love you cannot experience.

"That is not the worst," Chef said, adding another French phrase.

"Can you say it in English?" I asked.

He gave me a sad look, then said, "I love someone who can never be mine."

"You're right. That is sadder." I told Angeline what he'd said, adding, "I think he's still in love with Norma. She owned the house and restaurant when he was alive. I sense her presence at times."

She gave me a knowing look. "I think the woman he is in love with is very much alive. That is why he can't be with her."

"Oh." I gave that a moment of thought. Perhaps he'd always been in love with Helen, Jennifer's grand-mother. "Maybe they can be together in the future. I mean, if he's waited fifty years for her, what's a few more?" I glanced at Chef who now avoided making eye contact with me. "Sorry. Don't mean to talk about your love life behind your back. Or rather in front of you."

"I will leave you two alone to discuss the matter," Angeline gave me a kiss on each cheek and slipped out the back door.

Emile had faded from view. "Discuss the matter?" I muttered. "What does she mean by that?"

~

WHILE I DECIDED what to do with my extra free day, I took care of some of the weekly tasks I usually did on Mondays. After spending an hour upstairs on the computer entering numbers into the accounting program, my head began to throb. Peppermint tea sometimes helped with a headache, so I made my way downstairs to the kitchen where I found Freddie waiting for me without her usual upbeat personality.

"What's up?" I asked. "You don't seem like yourself."

"It's nothing." She stood by the sink and stared out the window obviously bothered by something.

"Are you worried about the earring?"

She swung around to face me. "Who told you about that?" Her voice oozed suspicion.

"No one." Maybe I should have kept that knowledge to myself.

"Wait." With one more glance outside, she pulled up a stool at the island. "You were in the room with Orson's body, weren't you? Is that how you knew about it?"

I nodded, putting the kettle on to boil. "My first instinct was to pick it up, but I didn't have the chance. That's probably a good thing—I wouldn't have wanted to get caught tampering with evidence. I hoped someone else had also worn gold hoops that day, and then I thought Angeline might have gone into the study and talked to Kaslov. But when she said she hadn't gone in the study…"

"Who told you that?" Freddie asked, an accusatory tone in her voice.

"She did, I think…" No, Chef had told me what he'd

overheard when Molina had interviewed Angeline. I could hardly tell Freddie that a ghost was my informant. Even when Irma had blurted out that I had a ghost, she laughed it off. "Um, I don't remember."

"If Molina is sharing information with you when he warned me not to do the exact same thing, I'm going to give him a piece of my mind."

"Don't do that," I said. "I think I overheard something I wasn't supposed to."

Freddie didn't let on whether she believed me or not. "I'm taking my mother to Monterey for the day. Maybe visit the aquarium. Try and stay out of trouble, will you?"

"When do I—?" I began, but her smirk stopped me. "I'm just going to stay home and try a new recipe. Someone has been leaving produce on my porch. This time they also left a recipe for chocolate beetroot cake."

"Beetroot?" she asked. "Aren't beets already roots?"

"We call the whole plant a beet, but I think it's a British recipe, and they use different terms. Maybe they want to make sure you don't put the leaves in too. Funny, though, that they don't call carrots 'carrot roots.'" I shrugged. "Also, I'm going to have to convert all the grams and milliliters. With the tearoom closed, I've got plenty of free time. And when I'm done baking, maybe I'll quietly and safely make a list of suspects."

"A list without my mother on it?" she asked.

"Exactly."

CHAPTER 5

$\mathcal{M}$y home had come with nearly every conceivable cooking tool and device including a kitchen scale. I'd planned to order a digital scale but hadn't gotten around to it, so I retrieved the old-fashioned one from the storeroom and set it on the kitchen counter.

It had a large bowl on top and a dial on the front that indicated both ounces and grams. The recipe I'd been given for chocolate beetroot cake listed British measurements which meant I'd be using the grams scale.

I put the beets on the scale first, then scrubbed them and popped them into a pot of boiling water. I could have peeled them first, but the peels would slip right off after they were cooked. I checked them with a fork after thirty minutes, but they still seemed firm, so I let them boil another ten minutes.

While the beets cooled, I double-checked the recipe.

200 ml of oil seemed like a lot, and I considered checking for other recipes online but reconsidered.

"You'll never know if you don't follow the recipe the way it's written," I told myself.

Chef appeared, perhaps thinking I spoke to him. "All of my recipes must be followed exactly to the letter."

"It's not your recipe," I explained. "I found it on my doorstep with some fresh beets. Someone in town must have a vegetable garden and they've been leaving me presents. This morning, I found beets and a recipe for chocolate cake that uses them."

Chef's expression indicated he didn't approve of my idea. "If you will refer to my cookbook, 'Modern French Cooking,' you will find a recipe for the most exquisite chocolate torte. I will assist you if you wish."

"Thanks," I said, "But I'd really like to try this out. I've been looking to eat more vegetables and adding them to chocolate cake sounds like a brilliant plan. That is if it tastes good." I had my doubts, but I was willing to give it a try. "Besides, I've already cooked the beets."

"Have it your way," he said as he faded from view.

"Great. Now I've offended you." Chef must have been used to people doing what he said when he was alive, but he'd have to get used to me having a mind of my own.

I began peeling the beets, being careful to keep the bright red juice in the sink. Luckily, I had an over-the-sink cutting board to use to chop them up. I rinsed off my hands and retrieved the blender from the cupboard and set it up next to the sink.

Adding the chopped beets to the blender, I pulsed them after every scoopful. The sound of the back door distracted me, and I hit pulse before replacing the lid. Beet puree shot out the top, spreading all over the counter and splashing onto my apron. I swung around, holding my juice-covered hands up in a vain attempt to keep beet juice from going everywhere.

"April!" Jennifer cried out the moment she saw me. "You've been hurt! I'll call 9-1-1. No, I'll get you a towel. Where is it bleeding?"

After looking at the front of my apron and my bright red hands, I understood her concern. I began to laugh as I tried to say, "I'm fine."

"You're not fine," Jennifer said.

By that point, I was laughing too hard to speak. "Beets," was all I could say. I pointed to the food processor until she finally figured out what I meant.

Jennifer's brows drew together, as irritation replaced panic when she realized I wasn't in any danger.

I gave her a sheepish grin. "Sorry. I didn't mean to freak you out."

Her mouth began to twitch. "You should see yourself," she said. She began chuckling as she grabbed her phone. "I'm getting a picture of this and it's going on my IG."

I let her take the picture. "Now will you help me clean up this mess?"

"No way," she said, still chuckling. "You're on your

own." She headed for the stairs but turned back when she reached the first step. "What are you making anyway?"

"Chocolate beetroot cake," I said.

She began to giggle. "I have a better name for it."

"What's that? I asked.

"Crime scene cake."

After cleaning up from my first attempt at what would now always be known as Crime Scene Cake, I cooked more beets and continued with the recipe.

I was about to put it in the oven when Jennifer returned to the kitchen.

"Oh good, the kitchen looks like a kitchen again." She swiped a finger into the bowl and tasted the batter. "Ugh."

"Ugh?" That wasn't a good sign. "What's wrong?"

"You taste it."

The moment I licked the batter I realized what I'd done wrong. I sighed. "I forgot the sugar." I scraped the batter back into the bowl, measured the sugar, and folded it in.

"You're dangerous," Jennifer said.

I ignored her and put the cake in the oven, hoping for the best. "I should know better than to try out a new recipe when I'm distracted."

"Why are you distracted?" Jennifer asked, but then she saw the look on my face. "Oh, right. The dead guy in the study." She headed for the back door. "Save some cake for me, please. I'm off to my grandma's. She's making Sunday dinner for me and my dad."

"You sure are milking this whole 'I have a grandma'

thing, aren't you?" I teased.

"You bet! Having a grandma is the best."

FIRST THING MONDAY MORNING, as I sipped my coffee, I checked the Friends of the Library used bookshop's hours. I'd stop there first and then swing by Featherman's bookshop. After a leisurely breakfast, I drove to the library, arriving at ten o'clock just as they opened.

Climbing the stone steps brought back memories, most of them pleasant ones. The time I thwarted the mayor's plan to gut the structure and turn it into a food court was my favorite.

The tiny library bookstore tucked away in a corner near the front of the building, held a large assortment of donated and retired books.

A figure crouched behind some boxes. I recognized the brown hair and bright orange shirt.

Quietly, hoping not to startle her, I softly called, "Harriet?"

Her head popped up. "Oh, hello."

"How are you?" I figured I'd start with some pleasantries before grilling her about her meeting with Kaslov.

"Oh, okay, I suppose. I hardly slept at all last night with my back hurting the way it has lately. I have an appointment later today. They'll probably do more x-rays and maybe give me a cortisone shot. It usually helps for a bit, but the pain always comes back. And those doctors' visits add up."

"Sorry to hear that." Before giving her a chance to list more of her ailments, I tried to steer the conversation in a different direction. "You've got a lot of books here."

"Yes, well, they're not my books, really, but I kind of feel like they are. Although if I could get someone to help move the boxes around, my back might not hurt so much."

"Uh-huh." Maybe the direct approach would be better after all. "So, about Saturday..."

She straightened up and her eyes widened. "What about Saturday."

"Why did you want a reading from The Amazing Kaslov when you said he was the devil."

"I didn't say that." She folded her arms over her chest. "And if I did, that's my business, don't you think? I don't ask you why you do the things you do."

"Yes, but if someone died, you might." I waited for a response which didn't come. "You looked pretty angry when you came out of the study after your reading."

She scowled. "I told the police everything I know."

"Yes, I figured as much. It's just—"

"I bet Angeline killed him," she blurted out. "She hated him. Everyone heard her threaten him. If her daughter wasn't the coroner, she'd probably already be arrested."

"You mean when Angeline gave Kaslov the reading he asked for? You heard her threaten him?"

"I sure did." Harriet wore a smug smile. "She said, 'Death is in your future.'"

"That sounds like a fortune, not a threat to me.

When you think about it, death is in all of our futures."

Her smile turned into a frown. "Then she said, 'And I'll make sure it's sooner rather than later.'"

"You heard her say that?" When she nodded, I asked, "And you told Deputy Molina this? Word for word?"

"I certainly did."

"You're a liar." I felt my blood pressure rise along with my anger. "You and I were in the kitchen when Angeline first started telling Kaslov's fortune, and then I watched you walk out the front door. You couldn't have heard more than a word or two."

She sputtered, hemmed, and hawed. "Everyone heard it."

"Maybe so. But you made up that last part. There are only two reasons why you're claiming that Angeline said that. One, you're out to get her. And two, it was you who murdered Kaslov." I paused, then added, "Maybe both."

"I'm not saying anything else to you," Harriet said, her face just as red and blotchy as when she'd emerged from the study the day of the murder.

"Fine." Without another word, I stormed out of the library. By the time I reached my car, unlocked it, and sat down behind the wheel, I began to regret losing my temper. Our talk might have been more productive if I'd stayed calm.

Before driving anywhere, I took a few deep breaths to calm myself. I wasn't sure what had made me angrier—the lie about overhearing Angeline threaten Kaslov or the thought that she would do something to hurt someone like Angeline.

Did I really think Harriet had murdered Kaslov? I had to admit to myself that it was unlikely. She might be feeling vulnerable after being questioned as a murder suspect and that might have led to her accusing Angeline.

I would have loved to have seen her reaction when she learned that the victim wasn't Kaslov after all, but I wasn't sure that information had been released to the public. I didn't need to get on Molina's bad side.

Once my heart rate and breathing had returned to normal, I drove to Featherman's bookstore and parked on the street in front of the gray brick building. I took the stone walkway to the glass-paneled front door and tried the handle. It turned, and I stepped inside.

I blinked and nearly stepped back outside to check that I was in the right shop. Gone were the dusty books stacked willy-nilly everywhere. Gone, too, were the cobwebs and the dim lighting that gave everything a dingy appearance.

Now, polished bookshelves full of neat rows of books stood on either side of a wide aisle. An open area in the back had been cleared of the boxes that had filled the space when I'd first visited.

Mr. Featherman emerged from an office dressed in his usual tweed jacket and greeted me. "April, how nice of you to stop by."

"I'm so impressed with the way you've transformed the shop." I gestured to the open space. "What are you planning to do with this part of the shop? Or are you waiting for more shelves to arrive?"

"I'm planning to do author signings, book clubs,

that sort of thing. And over here," he pointed to a nook with a miniature sofa and chairs, "is an area for children where there will be plenty of books and toys to occupy young readers."

Most of the antique furniture I'd seen before had been replaced by sturdy new pieces, but one lamp looked familiar. "You kept the Tiffany lamp."

"I did," he said, a wistful look in his eyes. "My father loved that lamp. As soon as I find a permanent place to live in town, I'll move it there. It's much too valuable to keep here in the shop."

"I'm glad you didn't have to sell it." While I tried to think of a way to transition to my questions about the day of the murder, I quietly moved around the room checking out the new decor.

Mr. Featherman watched me for a minute or two before he spoke and saved me from my awkwardness. "I know why you're here."

I swung around to face him and gave him a goofy smile. "Am I that transparent?"

"Let's have a seat, shall we?" He led me to a round table surrounded by wooden chairs that I guessed he planned to use for book club meetings. Once we were seated, he said, "I'm sorry to disappoint you, but I didn't see anything on Saturday. Nothing that might have anything to do with the murder."

"Oh." I'd hoped he had a clue that would help make sense of the information I'd learned so far. "If you don't mind, would you tell me what you saw anyway?"

He nodded and folded his hands on the table in front of him. "We all heard someone yell 'fire' outside, of course. The two other vendors and I didn't want to leave our merchandise when there didn't seem to be any imminent danger, so we stayed put. There were two young ladies who had been looking at candles and jewelry— "

"I think I remember them. The blonde one asked you about an author."

He chuckled. "Yes. I only brought esoteric and metaphysical books with me that day, the sort I thought might interest people visiting a psychic fair, but she wasn't interested in any of those."

"What did the two friends do when everyone ran outside?"

"Oh, I don't think they were friends," he said. "Although I'm hardly an expert on the subject. I got the feeling they happened to arrive around the same time. The blonde went to the door and came back to tell us that it was just a trashcan fire."

"And the other woman?"

He looked up for a moment as if recalling, then shook his head. "I think she may have gone outside with everyone else. Or she left. I don't recall seeing her again."

ON THE WAY home from the bookshop, I picked up tacos from the imaginatively named Taco Taco along with a couple of Mexican beers for Jennifer and me. Just as I got back in my car, Jennifer texted that she was going out with friends, which meant I had four tacos to eat by myself. When I arrived home, I unlocked the back door and went to put one of the beers in the refrigerator.

I heard a noise in the kitchen. Holding one of the beer bottles over my head ready to bash an intruder with it, I called out, "Is that you, Emile?" as I stepped through the door.

"Who's Emile?" Freddie asked, eying my bottle. "And what are you planning on doing with that?"

"Oh, nothing." I joined Freddie at the island and offered her the other beer, which she declined. "What are you doing here?"

"Jennifer let me in. She said you wouldn't be long." She watched me twist open my beer. "Maybe I will have one."

"And a taco?"

"I'm taking my mother out for dinner, but please go ahead without me."

Four tacos were way more than I could eat alone, so I split them between two plates and put them both on the island. "You don't have to eat them if you don't want to, but I bought them for Jennifer and I don't think they'll be very appetizing by the time she gets home."

"They do have really good tacos. I suppose just one wouldn't ruin my appetite." Freddie asked about my day while we ate.

"I stopped by the library," I said. "Checked out their little used bookstore."

"And I suppose you talked to Harriet? How is she?"

I tried not to look guilty. "She's fine."

She watched me as I took another bite of my taco, making me uncomfortable.

I swallowed and said, "What?"

Freddie smirked. "Just wondering what you're not telling me. Is it about the murder?"

"Sort of," I admitted.

"Is it about my mother?" Freddie asked.

I sighed. "Do they teach mind-reading at med school these days or did you learn it from your mother?"

"I can read you like an open book. You're a terrible liar, which is a good thing as far as I'm concerned. What did Harriet have to say?"

To buy time, I took a long sip of beer. Then a big bite of my taco which I chewed slowly. Finally, I decided not to delay the inevitable any longer. "Harriet told me what Angeline said when she read Kaslov's fortune. According to Harriet, she threatened him."

"Did she tell you exactly what my mother said?"

"See, that's the thing," I explained. "Harriet had left just before Angeline told Kaslov that death was in his future, but she told Molina that she overheard Angeline threaten Kaslov."

"A lot of people are saying that she threatened him," Freddie said with a sigh.

"Yes, but I don't like Harriet adding her voice to the mix when everything she said is hearsay. I have to tell Molina that her witness statement is a whole lot of hooey."

"I'll tell him." Freddie became quiet and I waited for her to say whatever she had on her mind. "But even if

Harriet didn't hear what she said to Kaslov, plenty of other people did."

"You're worried." I reached out to give her hand a reassuring pat.

"Well of course I am." She tapped her fingers against her bottle, and I could almost feel her agitation. "My mother threatened him not long before he was murdered."

"Plus, there's the earring," I said. "Do you think someone found the earring and then planted it in the study to implicate her?"

Freddie scratched at the label on her beer bottle with her fingernails. "That's something I'd like to know."

"What are we going to do?" I asked. One of the tacos sat on my plate untouched, but I wasn't hungry anymore. "Also, until we learn more about this Orson guy, it seems likely that he was killed because someone thought he was Kaslov. We can't just sit here and let someone else get killed."

"You think the real Kaslov is in danger?"

"Yeah, I think that's a real possibility. I'm not going to sit around and wait to find out, are you?"

She put her face in her hands and mumbled, "My mother is a murder suspect and I'm the coroner. I can't get involved."

"What are you talking about? You're going to follow the rules when people's lives are at stake?"

She looked up and gave me a scolding look. "You don't know how this works, April. Any evidence, any testimony that I uncover will be tainted because I'm her daughter. The best thing, the only thing I can do is to sit this one out. You have no idea how hard that is."

"Oh." I hadn't thought of that. I stood and carried our dishes to the sink. When I returned to my seat, I said, "Then tell me what to do. I'll be your eyes and ears and whatever other body parts you need."

That brought a hint of a smile to her face. "Go see Kaslov."

Before I could respond, a quick knock on the back door told me Irma had arrived. I glanced at the clock when she entered. "Don't you have a restaurant to run?"

She waved a hand at me. "I've got competent employees. They can do without me for an hour or so." She saw the takeout bag on the counter. "You guys had a taco party without me?"

"The party's not over yet. Have a seat." I handed her my untouched taco and nodded in Freddie's direction. "She wants me to visit The Amazing Kaslov and see what I can find out." I explained that Angeline was a suspect, so Freddie couldn't get involved in the investigation.

"You're going to the castle, huh?" Irma lifted one eyebrow.

I shrugged. "I would, but I don't see how I'm going to get in. He'll hardly talk to anyone. How am I supposed to get him to see me?"

Irma grinned. "You'll take me with you."

CHAPTER 6

I stared at Irma dumbfounded. "You know The Amazing Kaslov?"

"I knew him back before he was amazing. He was just okay back then." She paused waiting for my reaction. "That was a joke."

"Oh. Haha."

She sighed. "Some people have no sense of humor. Pick me up tomorrow morning around eight and I'll tell you all about me and Mr. Amazing." She got up to go.

"Wait," I called after her as she headed for the door. "Why'd you stop by?"

"I almost forgot. Do you have a meat grinder?"

"A meat grinder?" I repeated.

"I'm going to try making sausages from scratch. I don't want to buy a grinder until I decide if it's worth the trouble."

We went into the backroom to look together. When I'd bought my house, it had come complete with an amazing collection of cooking tools and utensils, many of which I had no idea what they were for.

"Is this a meat grinder?" I asked, holding up a contraption with a hand crank.

"That's a grain mill," Irma said. "At least I think that's what it is. But you're on the right track."

When we found the grinder, she grinned and said, "If it comes out good, I'll save you some. See you tomorrow."

"Bright and early," I called out after her.

When she opened the door and stepped outside into the darkening evening, the motion sensor light turned on illuminating the walkway. As she turned the corner, she called back, "Bring coffee."

WHEN THE ALARM went off the next morning, it took me a few moments to remember why I'd set it for such an early time. Then it hit me. If everything went as planned, I'd get to see the inside of the castle today, and maybe get some clues to Orson's death.

Irma's cornflower blue bungalow with white shutters sat smack in the middle of our little town, only ten blocks from me. I pulled into her driveway and walked to the red-painted front door. Sarah had talked her into the color, saying it would be good feng shui.

Irma answered the door. "If you have to pick me up this early, would you at least try not to act so dang cheerful?"

Irma's grouchy greeting transformed when she got

into the car where I had a caramel macchiato from Molly's bakery waiting for her. As I drove out of town toward Kaslov's home, I asked how she'd come to know him.

"I don't think he built the castle planning to be a recluse," she explained. "Just a vanity project for someone with more dollars than sense, in my opinion. But when all the fallout happened—"

"When is someone going to tell me what happened way back then?"

"I suppose now is as good a time as any." She stared out her window at the hills and trees passing by. "Where to begin?" She tapped her fingers on the armrest. "We'll be there in twenty minutes, so I'll give you the short version."

By the time we turned off the main road, Irma had brought me up to speed with Kaslov's career starting from touring the country, followed by talk show appearances, and ending up with his own television show. When he wasn't working on the show, he'd see clients who would spend hundreds of dollars to have their fortunes told by him, some flying in from all around the country or even the world.

"After Angeline graduated college and started grad school, she brought her sister from Haiti. She wanted Esther to have all the opportunities she did. When Esther began having debilitating headaches, she took her to see Dr. Severs. That's how they met each other, but that's another story. Anyway, Dr. Severs referred her to a specialist, but instead, she went to Kaslov. He told her she would live a long and happy life."

I had a feeling I knew where this was going. "But she didn't?"

Irma shook her head slowly. "By the time Freddie finally talked her into seeing a neurologist, the brain tumor was untreatable. She lasted less than a year."

"No wonder Angeline hates Kaslov so much." We drove in silence for several minutes before I remembered Irma hadn't told me how she knew Kaslov. "So, what's the story with you and the magician?"

"Mentalist," she corrected. "At least that's what he called himself." She shifted in her seat, and I wondered if the subject made her uncomfortable. "After Esther died, he went into seclusion. Mind you, I don't know if that's why he decided to withdraw from society, but it was around the same time. He didn't have a cook, and that was before there were apps on your phone to order dinner. Take out meant Chinese food or pizza, and even they didn't like to deliver all the way out here."

The narrow road curved through the woods, and my mind went back to the first time I'd driven up here, just weeks ago. "He talked you into delivering food from your restaurant?"

"Not exactly. I came up here every Monday morning and cooked a week's worth of food for him and later for him and Theadora."

"Who's Theadora?" I asked.

"His sister. Sometime in the late nineties, I think it was, her husband passed away. Theadora was about six months pregnant when she came to live with him. She died in childbirth."

"How sad." I remembered the woman I'd seen walking the grounds. She'd be around the right age. "So, he raised her daughter Thea?"

"You know about Thea?"

"I saw her when I was here before. She seemed almost..." I tried to come up with the right word. "Otherworldly."

She chuckled. "That's a good way to describe her. People always said she was slow, but I don't think that was it. Kaslov sent her to kindergarten in Somerton—it was the closest elementary school—but after the first year, he pulled her out and subjected her to a series of nannies, governesses, and tutors. As far as Kaslov was concerned, each one was a disappointment except for Martha who still lives with them I believe."

"How long did you cook for Kaslov?" I asked.

"Almost ten years. When Martha arrived to be Thea's tutor, he found out she was a decent cook, so she took over the responsibility. He liked to keep a minimal staff, both for efficiency and to protect his privacy. When anyone applied for a position, he always suspected they wanted to sell a story to the tabloids or get exclusive photos. Locking yourself away in a castle can make a person paranoid, apparently."

The road took a sharp turn to the left and the castle came into view at the top of the hill. It stood majestic as any fairy tale castle, and like many of the stories I read as a child, it seemed the residents did not live happy lives.

As we pulled up to the gate, it opened, and I drove through. A paved driveway led to an area that seemed designed for visitors to park, even though Kaslov had few visitors from what Irma had told me.

I got out of the car and took in the impressive sight of the gray stone castle as I walked toward the entrance. "There *is* a moat," I exclaimed. "I couldn't see it from the gate the other day."

"I suppose you can call it that. But there's no draw-bridge," Irma noted.

A murky pond encircled the structure like a moat. Thick with lily pads and bordered by reeds, I leaned over the side to see if any fish swam in the dark water.

"Come on." Irma led the way to a stone footbridge that crossed the moat to the enormous wooden front door. I examined the brass door knocker, an Art Deco design in the shape of a dragon. As I reached for it, the door swung open.

The woman I now knew as Kaslov's niece, Thea, stood at the door in the same multi-colored robe draped over an off-white blouse and loose pants. Her porcelain skin appeared even more flawless up close. Her hair, pulled back into a tight bun, gave her a stern appearance, reminding me of a stereotypically strict librarian.

And those red lips! Did she put on lipstick the moment she got out of bed?

She blinked lazily and spoke as if bored. "Who are you?"

"You know who I am." Irma didn't try to hide her annoyance. "Tell your uncle I'm here to see him."

Thea stared at Irma with no recognition, then gave me the same non-expression. "And who are you?"

"Hi!" I said cheerfully. "I'm April May. You must be Thea. I own the SereniTea Tearoom—just opened a few months ago. You should stop by sometime for afternoon tea. Ow."

Irma had jabbed me with a sharp elbow. I bet she'd be great in a street fight.

I took the hint and got to the point. "We're here to see Mr. Kaslov."

Thea sighed then turned and shuffled away. As she did, her robe trailed behind her, but now I realized it was a luxurious, full-length velveteen coat. She left the door open, so we followed her inside.

The interior was the same gray stone as the exterior as if the entire home had been built of solid rock. I stroked a finger across the wall, expecting the feel of a faux veneer, but it felt cold and rough.

"No touching," Irma muttered.

I whispered back, "This place is like a real castle. It must have cost a fortune."

My feet sunk into thick rugs covering most of the stone floors. We entered a cavernous room, and I shivered. "It's freezing in here." No wonder Thea wore a coat indoors.

Flames crackled in the fireplace, but it wasn't enough to warm the oversized room with ceilings reaching twenty or thirty feet high. Wall sconces gave off a warm glow along with thin beams of sunlight that filtered in through tall thin leaded glass windows.

Thea was nowhere to be found. I stood on a deep blue carpet with stars woven in. Being trampled on over the years hadn't diminished its beauty.

I spun around at the sound of a door opening behind me. A plump woman around my age entered wearing an apron and a broad smile.

"Irma!" She scurried over to us, her salt and pepper bob bouncing.

The two women hugged, and it seemed as if the woman might suffocate tiny Irma. They began chattering, both talking at the same time. I had no idea what they said, but I waited patiently for them to catch up.

Irma acknowledged my presence. "This is my new friend April," she said. "Meet Martha."

"Lovely to meet you," she shook my hand vigorously, then turned back to Irma. "Since when did you have friends?"

Irma laughed. "Including you, Martha, that makes two. That is if you admit to being a friend of mine."

"Don't be silly," Martha said with a grin. "What brings you here today? It doesn't have anything to do with Orson, does it?"

"You know him?" I asked.

"Know him! He worked here for the past three years." She sighed. "Such a nice man. We all liked him, especially Thea. A little too much perhaps, but what do you expect when you shut up a young girl and don't allow her to have a boyfriend her own age."

"True," Irma said. "Kaslov didn't like them getting close?"

She scoffed. "He confided in me that he planned to fire Orson. I'm not sure what he was waiting for." She shook her head. "Here I am gossiping with you two when the master is waiting for you. I'll show you the way."

I leaned over and whispered to Irma. "Master?" She gave me a knowing nod in response.

Martha led us down a narrow hallway. She opened the door and stepped aside. "Good luck," she whispered as we entered.

I held back a gasp. Starry lights twinkled from every surface of the round room except the domed ceiling where a mural depicted the constellations of the zodiac. The artist had represented my sign, Gemini, with two dark-haired women, and I recognized several other signs such as the archer and the goat.

I pulled my gaze away from the ceiling to the man standing by the large picture window. He didn't acknowledge our presence, instead gazing at the wild and untamed grounds and the ocean beyond. He sighed, stepped away from the window, and approached us. Kaslov resembled Orson superficially— medium build, gray hair, dark eyes, but Kaslov's eyes had a haunted look. He wore a long, velveteen cloak in the same pattern as Thea's. The fire in the fireplace did little to alleviate the chill.

A movement in one corner caught my eye. Another dark-haired woman, around the same age as Thea, gave a start. I quickly looked away, pretending I hadn't seen her. Seeing ghosts was starting to become a habit, one I wasn't sure I liked.

The woman spoke softly. "You can see me?"

I ignored her and nudged Irma, who gave me a dirty look, but seemed to get my hint.

"Nice to see you, Kaz," she said. "It's been a while."

The Amazing Kaslov chuckled. "You're the only one who gets away with calling me that." His smile faded away. "I assume this isn't a social call."

"Nope, 'fraid not," Irma said, blunt as always.

Kaslov motioned to chairs arranged in front of the fire, and I gratefully took one, reaching my hands out toward the flames to warm them.

Kaslov removed his cloak and laid it over one of the chairs before sitting. He gestured to the chair between us for Irma. She plopped down obediently.

"An officer arrived at my gate late Saturday night," Kaslov said. "He asked me about Orson. I assume that's why you are here, Irma. Always the curious one, sticking your nose where it doesn't belong."

"My nose belongs wherever I want it to go," Irma said, adding to me, "It must have been Deputy Molina." She turned back to Kaslov. "Is that all the officer did? Ask you a few questions?"

For a moment, I wasn't sure he would answer, then he said, "Yes. Including asking me to search the premises."

"And did you allow that?" Irma asked.

"I have nothing to hide," Kaslov said.

"Besides, if you said no, he'd just go get a search warrant."

I jumped in before their bickering turned into an argument. "We're also here to warn you. If the person who killed Orson thought he was you, then they haven't achieved what they intended. You could be in danger."

He smiled as if he hadn't heard or understood my words. He gave a wide sweeping gesture with his arm. "Do you truly believe danger can reach me here?"

Irma huffed. "Danger can reach you anywhere. Keeping yourself and Thea cooped up within these stone walls has not kept you safe. It's kept you isolated and turned her into an agoraphobe."

His eyes narrowed and the tension in the room thickened. "How dare you tell me what's best for my niece."

I jumped in. "Can we get back to Orson and how your life might be in danger? Did you know that Orson had planned to impersonate you at my event?"

His eyes reluctantly left Irma as he trained his attention on me. "I didn't even know about your event. I suppose he wanted a taste of my fame and glory."

"And money," Irma added.

"Did you know he had a record?" I asked.

He nodded. "I believe people deserve a second chance. Everyone I hire has a need to redeem themselves. Even you, Irma. When I hired you to cook for me, you were full of resentment. You felt you'd been betrayed."

"I *was* betrayed," Irma corrected him with a grim smile.

"Be that as it may be," Kaslov said, his voice gentle, "your heart was full of revenge, but I also saw the capacity in you to, if not forgive, at least move past your bitterness."

"But Orson was a thief, not someone hurt and angry," I said.

"Ah but there you would be wrong." Kaslov stared into the fire, seemingly lost in thought. "The source of nearly every bad deed is hurt, anger, or both. So many of us are haunted by our past, and we need some time away from the world to heal."

I glanced at the ghost who hadn't moved from where I'd first spotted her. She watched Kaslov with a look of such sadness it caught my breath. I averted my eyes but not quickly enough.

"You *can* see me," she said. "Don't deny it." She must have noticed my grimace, because she added, "If you can see me, you can help me. Us."

I sighed. This whole ghost-whisperer stuff was getting old. I had enough to worry about without taking on the problems of the spirit world. Doing my best to ignore the pleading ghost, I tried to return to the conversation. What had we been talking about? Oh, right. Orson.

"Whatever Orson's reason," I said, "he impersonated you to bilk people out of their hard-earned money. Any idea why he would do that?"

Kaslov shook his head. "I paid him well."

"For what, exactly," Irma asked. When Kaslov answered with a raised eyebrow, she clarified, "What was his job here?"

Kaslov gave this a moment of thought before answering. "A little of everything, I suppose. His official title was butler, but since I rarely receive visitors, he took care of odd jobs around the house, helping Martha with the cleaning, running errands, things like that."

While they talked, I set my phone behind me on the chair, doing my best to be sneaky about it. Irma noticed what I was doing, and I gave her a little shake of my head, hoping she'd drop it until I could explain later.

It didn't seem as though we were getting anywhere. Irma tried to convince Kaslov his life might be in danger, and I did my best to ferret out clues to Orson's murder. He either knew little else about Orson, or he chose to keep the information to himself.

Finally, Irma stood. "We've taken up enough of your time. Thank you for seeing us."

I stayed seated. "One more question. Why would someone want to kill you?"

Kaslov and Irma both stared at me. Kaslov spoke first. "I have no idea. Unless..."

"Yes?" I prompted.

"Unless Angeline has not yet forgiven me."

CHAPTER 7

*K*aslov escorted us down the hall, and we'd nearly reached the main room when I said, "Oh no. My phone. I must have left it in the room."

Before Kaslov could object, I took off down the hall, hoping to get a moment alone with the ghost. I burst into the room and the ghost, wide-eyed, stared at me.

"You came back," she said.

"I don't have much time," I said. "You're Theadora, right?"

She nodded. "I need your help."

"Can you be a little more specific?" I gave her a gesture to hurry up while retrieving my phone from the chair.

"If something happens to my brother, Thea will be alone. I don't know if she can make it on her own."

I wanted to ask her why a seemingly healthy young woman couldn't get by without her uncle, especially considering she'd likely inherit his estate and wealth. I also wanted to know why Thea was cooped up in this house with an old man and a cook. But I didn't have time.

Instead, I asked, "Do you think something's going to happen to Kaslov?"

"Yes. Something bad."

Footsteps came closer and the door opened. Kaslov glared at me, so I showed him my phone. "Found it."

He spoke coolly. "Do you now have all your belongings, Ms. May?"

"Yep." I gave Theadora a shrug before following Kaslov down the hall. If only I could find a way to get more time with her, but how?

~

"WHAT WAS THAT ALL ABOUT?" Irma asked as we drove away from the castle.

"Huh?"

"The bit with the phone," she said. "Why did you want to be alone in that room. Did you see a clue?"

"A ghost," I said, thankful I'd convinced Irma that I actually did see ghosts. At first, I thought there was a special reason I could see Chef Emile, but now it appeared to be a general skill. "I hope I don't start seeing them everywhere I go."

"Whose ghost was it?"

"Theadora. She's worried about Kaslov, though actually, I think it's Thea she's really worried about.

She doesn't seem to think her daughter can take care of herself. Maybe if they gave her half a chance—"

"Maybe if they sent her off to college." Irma tapped the side of her head. "I have a feeling there's more going on in Thea's brain than anyone knows. When Theadora was in labor, Kaslov wouldn't take her to the hospital, and from what I understand it was a difficult birth. Thea had some difficulties as a small child, but I think her biggest problem has been people treating her like a porcelain doll."

"Oh." Thea seemed to be in her own world, but I saw intelligence in her eyes. "She seemed different to me, but has Kaslov ever had her tested?"

"You'd have to ask Freddie about that. But you know, brains aren't everything. I've known plenty of smart people who are miserable. Thea was such a sweet little girl who brought me flowers she picked in the garden. Never talked much, but when she was happy, she'd dance and sing, twirling around the room."

"She barely acknowledged you when she let us in, almost like she didn't recognize you."

"Oh, she recognized me all right."

I DROPPED Irma off at the Mermaid Cafe so she could get ready to open. It felt like it had already been a long day, and it wasn't even ten o'clock. All I wanted to do was put on a pair of sweats and eat lunch, but I had a tearoom to run.

I needed some time to process what Kaslov and the ghost of Theadora had told me, but first I had to let Freddie know what we learned on our visit to The Amazing Kaslov. I sent her a text.

When I stepped into the kitchen, Chef Emile leaned against the counter sipping wine.

"That wine looks good, but it's a little early in the day for it, don't you think?" He ignored me, and I glanced at the clock. "Wow, it's later than I thought." My stomach growled, reminding me I'd planned to make something to eat.

I checked the crisper bin where some vegetables were getting ready to go bad. I turned to Chef. "What can I do with parsnips and carrots?"

"They are root vegetables, as are potatoes, rutabagas, turnips..."

I interrupted his list. "Okay, thanks. What do I do with them?"

"As I was about to explain, root vegetables may be roasted or boiled for soup. If you plan to make soup, I recommend pureeing your vegetables and adding *crème liquide.*"

"Liquid cream?" I said, guessing at the translation. "You mean like heavy cream?"

"Americans," he scoffed, as if he hadn't already revealed to me that he had been born in Louisiana and was just as American as I was, French accent notwithstanding.

I'd tried to put on a pair of jeans that morning but couldn't zip them up. I'd give milk a try instead, and I wouldn't mention it to Chef. After all, why take a healthy soup and add several grams of fat to it? I sighed, knowing the answer—because it would be delicious.

While the parsnips and carrots boiled, I turned my back to Chef and poured some milk into a pitcher. He'd never know the difference.

Freddie arrived as I finished pureeing the soup but turned down my offer to share a bowl with me. I reheated a few sweet potato biscuits on a cookie sheet.

"I'll take one of those," Freddie said, pointing to the biscuits. I handed her one and she broke it open, slathering butter on the flaky surface. She took a bite and gave me her verdict. "Yum."

I carried my soup and biscuits to my favorite seat in front of the fireplace. "A fire would be nice," I said, "but I'm too tired to build one." Now that summer had nearly come to an end, there was a nip in the air, especially on an overcast day like today.

"I'll do it." Before I could stop her, she'd piled two logs on the andirons and lit the gas. "See. Easy."

"Thanks. The castle was so cold, I can still feel the chill in my bones."

"I know what you mean," Freddie said. "I always bring a sweater or jacket when I make house calls."

"When you visit Kaslov, do you see Thea too?"

Freddie gave me a scolding look. "You know I can't tell you anything about my patients."

"I already know that Kaslov thinks something's not right with her and blames himself since he didn't take his sister to the hospital to have her baby. But I don't think there's anything wrong with her intelligence."

"Did you learn anything about Orson?" Freddie asked, changing the subject.

"Martha, the cook, thinks he was about to be fired because he was getting too close to Thea, if you know what I mean."

Freddie sighed. "I told Kaslov she needs to be around people her age. It's almost like he doesn't want her to have a life of her own."

I nodded, wondering if she felt like a prisoner in her home. "Maybe he's afraid if she met someone, she'd leave him, and he'd be alone."

She frowned. "Nothing is keeping him a shut-in except himself. If he would just go see a therapist, he might—" She stopped, realizing she'd said too much. "Anyway, there's no reason for Thea to be stuck there with just an old man and some servants for company."

I couldn't tell her what Theadora's mother had said to me, since I'd never told Freddie about Chef Emile or any other ghosts I'd seen. She didn't strike me as the sort of person who would believe in ghosts, so I wasn't in any hurry to tell her now.

"I can see you thinking," Freddie said. "What aren't you telling me?"

I hesitated. "Just that some people seem to think Kaslov might be in danger."

She gave me a questioning look. "Some people?"

"If someone killed Orson thinking he was Kaslov, then they're not necessarily just going to give up. He might be the next victim."

"The murderer must have thought Orson was Kaslov," Freddie said. "No one here knew Orson, so who would have had a motive to kill him?"

"Only one person I can think of," I said. "The Amazing Kaslov."

"You think that Kaslov came here undetected and killed Orson?"

I shrugged. "I've heard of crazier things. Or maybe he hired someone. He couldn't exactly kill him in his own home. I mean, he could, but he'd have to bury him in his backyard, and that's never a good long-term solution."

"Why wouldn't he just fire him?" Freddie asked.

"I don't know." Did I have to figure out everything myself? "Maybe he was afraid Orson would talk Thea into leaving with him. We just agreed he was terrified of being alone."

"I'm not sure terrified is the right word, but I get your point." Freddie leaned back in her chair, deep in thought. She shook her head. "Kaslov is too smart and creative. He'd think of another way to get rid of Orson —something less risky."

"You may be right, but then we're back to square one." My mind swirled with ideas, none of them making any sense. "A cup of tea might help me think better. Want one?"

Freddie followed me into the kitchen where I filled the kettle and set it on the stove. While it heated up, I dug through the junk drawer for a pad of paper and a pen which I laid on the island.

At the top of the pad, I wrote "suspects" in big

letters. "So, we're back to the theory that someone killed Orson by mistake thinking he was Kaslov. Who had a motive to kill Kaslov?"

"Besides my mother, you mean?" Freddie smirked. "We have to write Angeline's name on the list. She's a suspect and we need to cross her off as soon as possible."

I dutifully wrote Angeline's name at the top. "Harriet's first on *my* list." I wrote the name down next on the notepad. "When I saw her come out of the study with her face red and blotchy, she looked like she could kill someone."

"But did she look like someone who had just done the deed? Or do you think she might have gone back in later when the trashcan caught on fire?"

"That's right, the trashcan." I'd forgotten about the fire. "Do you think the murderer set it on fire as a distraction?"

"I assumed so. Didn't you?"

"It makes sense," I agreed. "Does Molina know how the fire started?"

"If he does, he's not telling me. He's not sharing any details about the case with me. I'm the daughter of his prime suspect."

"Oh, right." I stared at the paper. "Who else should go on this list?"

"How about Sarah?" Freddie asked.

"Sarah?" Maybe I'd heard her wrong or maybe there was another Sarah I didn't know about. Cute, bubbly Sarah a murderer? "Sarah from the B&B? But she found the body."

"That doesn't mean she didn't kill him. Think about it. You've just killed someone and there are a bunch of people about to see you leave the room. There's no way you'd get away with it, so you scream and tell everyone you happened to find him on the floor."

"But Sarah?" I shook my head wondering if I was that bad of a judge of character. Then a memory popped into my head. "I've got a better suspect for you. Her husband."

"That milquetoast of a man?" Freddie stood next to me and read the name I'd just added. "His name is Simon?"

"You should have seen him when he arrived and caught Kaslov, or the person we thought was Kaslov anyway, flirting with his wife. And Sarah looked like she was enjoying it too. If I hadn't seen it with my own eyes, I wouldn't have believed Simon was capable of that much anger."

A rap on the door interrupted our list making, followed by Angeline's appearance. I flipped the notepad over and did my best to appear casual.

"Oh, good. You got my message," Freddie said. "Ready to go to dinner?"

Angeline's eyes darted from Freddie to me. "By the look on both your faces, I'm wondering if this is going to be my last supper."

I forced myself to smile. "No way. You have nothing to worry about."

Angeline narrowed her eyes at me, just the way her daughter had done so many times. "Then why are you trying to keep me from seeing that list you have?"

"Come on, Mama." Freddie took her mother by the arm. "I'm hungry."

~

I CARRIED a scoop of cat food along with a cup of water to the attic. Whisk, the Bengal cat who lived in my attic, was a surprisingly good listener.

Whisk sounded one high-pitched mew in greeting. Once his bowls were refilled, I took a seat in his favorite Windsor chair and watched him eat while I let my mind wander.

"Here's what I'm thinking, Whisk." His tail twitched at the sound of his name. "Sarah's husband Simon set the trash can on fire, then went into the study to kill the man he thought was Kaslov. Maybe Sarah saw him go in. No..." I pictured the scene in my mind. "More likely she saw him come out of the study, and when she saw the look on his face, she went in to find out what he'd done. Then, seeing the dead body, she did a quick search for clues, then screamed."

Whisk stopped eating and gazed at me intently for several seconds. Then he sat and began licking one of his front paws.

"Or." I tapped my fingers on the arm of the chair. "She was in on it."

Whisk must have finished the first paw, because he moved on to the other.

I shook my head. "No, scratch that. Sarah had no motive to kill Kaslov or Orson. Let's go back to the original theory. It makes the most sense."

I leaned back in the chair, and the cat made a trilling noise.

"Sorry, just thinking. We have other suspects. Angeline, of course, because she threatened him, but we know she didn't do it."

"Meow?"

"You can't think that the woman who raised a wonderful person like Freddie could be a murderer, do you? Besides, she has control over her emotions. She never would have let herself get in such a rage that she could do such a thing. Although her earring was found in the room, and she claimed she hadn't gone into the study. Oh! Maybe Sarah planted the earring to throw suspicion on someone other than Simon."

Whisk rubbed up against my leg then turned around and rubbed the other side before flopping on my feet.

"There's also Harriet, who said he was the devil. Of course, all this assumes that the murderer thought they were killing Kaslov. If someone knew his true identity, then I haven't a clue. Do you?"

Whisk startled me by jumping up on my lap where he took several turns before curling up. He didn't show me affection that often, so I sat still and enjoyed the feel of his weight and the soft vibration of his purring.

If the person who killed Orson wanted him dead because of something he'd done and not because they thought he was Kaslov, it must not have been anyone from our little community of Serenity Cove. No one even knew the man.

It had to be someone from the castle.

But if the person who killed Orson had intended to kill Kaslov, then Kaslov was still in danger.

Either way, I needed to make a repeat visit to the castle.

CHAPTER 8

The next morning, a knock on the door awoke me. I glanced at the clock. Why would Jennifer wake me up so early?

"What is it?" I called out.

"Sorry to wake you," Jennifer said through the door. "Irma is here asking for you."

What was Irma doing her so early? "I'll be right down."

After dressing and making my way downstairs, I entered the kitchen to find Irma at the island with a big mug of coffee. Jennifer handed me a cappuccino, and I gave her a grateful smile.

"Freddie sent me over," Irma whispered. "She wants us to go question Sarah. It's on the down-low."

"I can hear you, you know," Jennifer said. "What does 'on the down-low' mean?"

"It's a secret," Irma said.

"Fine," Jennifer sulked. "Don't tell me." She took her coffee and headed for the other room.

"That's what it means…" I began, but she'd already left. I'd explain later, but now I turned my attention back to Irma. "So did Freddie tell you to come get me at the crack of dawn?"

She smacked me on the leg. "Quit whining and let's go."

"What's in the bag," I asked.

"I almost forgot." Irma took a plastic container from the bag. "The sausage came out great, so I figured I'd bring some for Sarah. This one's for you, so stop complaining I never give you anything."

"When have I ever?" I began but decided to drop it.

I convinced Irma to walk since the Bed and Breakfast was only a few blocks away. She pulled a cap on her head and buttoned up her jacket as if she might freeze to death in the sixty-five-degree weather.

She rubbed her hands together. "Brrrr."

I laughed. "Save the dramatics for your next audition at the local theater."

"We don't have a local theater," Irma said. "Although I was once Scrooge at the annual Christmas show at the community center."

"Talk about typecasting."

We climbed the front steps of the Serenity Cove Bed and Breakfast. I held the door open for Irma, then followed her into the cozy interior. Sarah's favorite color, pink, predominated, but she managed to make it look tasteful.

Something had just come out of the oven, judging by the aroma of baked goods. "I smell cinnamon."

We walked through the parlor and just as we

stepped into the dining room, Sarah emerged from the kitchen carrying a tray. The scent of cinnamon and vanilla drifted over to us making my mouth water.

"Irma, April, how lovely of you to visit." She put the tray on the sideboard and gave us each a hug. "What brings you here?" Her smile faded as the realization must have hit her. "Oh, right. Everyone wants to talk to me about the dead guy. Did you two know that he was an imposter?"

"Not at the time," I assured her. "Came as quite a surprise to me."

Irma shrugged. "If I'd been there, I'd have known right away, but I was busy at the café with a wedding reception. And I am sorry, but yes, we're here to ask you about the dead guy. Freddie can't investigate herself because her mother is a suspect. She might be the only suspect that Molina has for all we know. But as long as we're here..." Her gaze drifted in the direction of the buffet and the tray of cinnamon rolls.

"Help yourself," Sarah said. "We only have one couple staying with us for the next couple of days. There's no way they could eat them all by themselves, even with my help."

Irma and I each put a gooey cinnamon roll on a plate and joined Sarah at a round oak table where cups of freshly poured coffee waited for us. After setting a sugar bowl and creamer in front of us, she asked, "What did you want to know?"

I eyed the roll dripping with icing hungrily, but since Irma had just taken a huge bite, I'd have to do the talking for starters. "We're trying to put together a timeline and figure out where everyone was when the fire broke out in the trash can outside. We figure that must have been when the murder happened. I was walking to the kitchen when Harriet came out of the study. Then I heard someone yell 'fire'. Do you remember where you were at the time?"

She answered quickly. "I was at my table by myself. I'd just given a reading to a young lady. She couldn't have been much more than a teenager, and she wanted to know what the future had in store for her. The cards showed a long and happy life, but she seemed disappointed when I told her that, so I added that the long and happy life would only occur after she'd overcome great adversity. For some reason, she was quite pleased at that."

"Was the young woman a blonde or brunette?" I asked, remembering the two women I'd seen talking to Mr. Featherman.

"She was the blonde," Sarah said. "I asked the other if she wanted a reading, but she said she had her life figured out. Funny thing for someone so young to say, don't you think? Although I went to school with a girl who knew she wanted to be a nurse in third grade. She's an R.N. now. I had no clue what I wanted to do at that age."

"Did you run outside when the fire started?" Irma asked, getting impatient with Sarah's chattiness.

"No," Sarah said, staring into her coffee cup. "I didn't see any reason with everyone else running outside. I mean, I figured I'd just get in the way."

"Of course," I said. "Do you remember who else was around when I was outside putting out the fire?"

"Well," she bit her lip as she thought over her answer. "Mr. Featherman stayed at his table, and so did the other two vendors. I don't know their names."

"And your husband?" I asked. "Did he stay with you?"

"My husband?" Her eyes widened. "He only stopped by to say hello and then he had to hurry back here. Fran covered for him for a little bit, but we like to always have one of us on the premises. You never know what sort of crisis might happen."

"Of course." I struggled to understand why she seemed so defensive. "I'm just hoping to find someone who might have seen or heard something. If they didn't realize the significance of what they saw, they might not have mentioned it to the police."

"Oh, I see." She stood as a middle-aged couple came down the stairs. "I'll be right back."

"Take your time." I bit into the roll, and it didn't disappoint with its gooey icing and soft, doughy texture. I sighed with contentment.

Sarah greeted the couple, offering them coffee and rolls and showing them to a table on the other side of the room.

"Does she seem nervous to you?" Irma asked in a whisper.

I nodded, my mouth too full to speak. After taking a swig of coffee, I said, "I wonder if something's going on with Simon and her. Or she might just be unnerved about Orson's death. I mean, she did see his body on the floor with a knife sticking out of it. She might want to forget that sight."

After serving her guests, Sarah returned to our table with two more rolls. I'd be eating salad for lunch for the rest of the month in a futile attempt to compensate for all the calories in this one breakfast. It was totally worth it.

She sat back down, appearing more composed. "Is there anything else I can tell you? I have to admit that I'm not the most observant person. Simon teases me about it all the time. I'm always forgetting where I put my keys. And I can never remember our guests' names. Lucky for me, Simon remembers everything."

"Did you see anyone go into or out of the study at the time of the fire?"

"I think I saw Harriet, but I think that was earlier. I didn't see anyone else. We were all watching out the window while you put out the fire."

"Of course," I stood, reluctant to leave the second roll behind. "Thanks for the information. I can only imagine what a shock it must have been to find him on the floor like that. If you need anything, let me know."

"Me, too." Irma stood also. "Stop by the Mermaid Cafe some evening and I'll buy you a glass of wine."

"You'll want to take those with you." Sarah hurried out of the room, returning with boxes.

We said our goodbyes and stepped onto the front porch.

"Yep," Irma said. "She's definitely hiding something."

"When did you become so suspicious?" I asked. "Sarah is a very nice lady, and I can't imagine her hurting a fly much less killing someone. Not everyone is comfortable talking about murder."

"I suppose so." Irma led the way back to my house. "Besides, if she wanted someone dead, she'd probably just poison one of her baked goods."

I decided to stay on Sarah's good side just to be safe. I'd hate to have to give up eating her delicious cinnamon rolls and muffins.

Irma and I said our goodbyes, and I tentatively accepted her invitation to stop by the cafe after work. When I stepped inside the house planning to get my car keys and drive back to the castle, the clock told me it was nearly time to open for lunch. My talk with Kaslov would have to wait.

Jennifer had set up for the day, with tiered trays and silverware wrapped up in napkins ready to go. She stood by the sink cutting cucumbers for tea sandwiches. "How many do you think we need for today?"

"It's hard to say." Now that all the schools were back in session, we had officially entered off-season. We had a few regulars who stopped by for lunch, but I could never predict how many people would stop in for afternoon tea. "The cucumbers will keep for at least a few days in water."

"And the deviled eggs will last until tomorrow morning when Irma stops by," Jennifer said with a grin. "How'd your visit with Sarah go?"

"Not sure." I didn't know how much I wanted to tell her about our investigation. "She didn't see much of anything."

"Well, there was a lot going on, like the fire?" She

put the containers full of sliced cucumbers into the refrigerator. "Now what?"

Getting a dozen hard-boiled eggs from the refrigerator, I handed her half of them. We stood over the sink to peel them, one of my least favorite tasks. I'd tried every method I could find on the internet, but nothing seemed to work any better than my mother's trick of rolling the eggs until the shells were nearly pulverized. If I planned to turn them into egg salad it didn't matter how they looked, which was a good thing. The ones that survived intact I set aside for deviled eggs.

Jennifer chopped eggs while I measured mayonnaise, Dijon mustard, and sea salt and mixed it all together. A quick taste told me the egg salad was perfect. Jennifer agreed.

I cut several slices of bread into circles and Jennifer buttered them. I liked to make the egg salad sandwiches round to add variety. We'd wait to assemble them, so they didn't get soggy. I sliced the crusts off more bread slices for cucumber and chicken salad sandwiches, which would be cut into triangles. Last of all were the open-faced smoked salmon sandwiches. It wasn't good enough for everything to taste delicious, I wanted it to be an artful display as well.

A pot of Coq au Vin simmering on the stove would be today's special with parsnip and carrot soup our soup du jour.

It occurred to me I hadn't asked Jennifer what she'd observed. "Did you see anything suspicious on Saturday?"

"Me?" She tilted her head to one side. "The fire was pretty suspicious, now that I think of it."

"I meant other than the fire. And the murder."

She shook her head. "I ran outside with everyone else."

I shrugged. "Not everyone. Sarah and Mr. Featherman and a few others stayed inside, but none of them saw anything. Or if they did, they don't know what they saw."

"Or they're not telling you," Jennifer suggested.

"That's a good point." I sighed. Investigating murder was hard enough without people keeping secrets from me.

Two couples stopped in for lunch shortly after we opened, but after they left, the tearoom was empty for the next hour. I spent the time making an English trifle, something I'd always wanted to do. I'd baked the cake the day before, so now all I had to do was make the custard and assemble everything.

I smiled at my optimism which I hoped wasn't misplaced. Nearly every recipe I'd tried lately that required custard had been a flop, but I wasn't going to let that stop me. Taking it slowly, I read every instruction twice. After an hour in the refrigerator, I took the custard out and tasted it. Much to my relief, it tasted delicious. Soon I had a beautiful glass bowl filled with layers of cake, custard, strawberries, and cream.

Late in the afternoon, three sisters arrived with

their mother for afternoon tea. When I learned that it was the mother's birthday, I suggested the SereniTea Queen's Afternoon Tea with champagne.

As I cleared their plates, I announced I had something special for them. I pulled the bowl of trifle from the refrigerator and scooped four servings, putting a candle in the middle of the mother's bowl, happy to see that it stayed in place.

We all sang "Happy Birthday" and they dug into their trifle. They gobbled it down and complimented me on it along with the rest of their meal. When they left, Jennifer and I were alone again.

"We've got to figure out how to get more people coming in during the off season," I said as I carried the last of the plates to the kitchen. "Or maybe cut back to three days a week."

"Oh," Jennifer said, sounding concerned. "What would you do with the free time?"

"Don't worry. I'll keep you busy forty hours a week as long as you want to keep working here. But it might be nice to try my hand at something else. Something creative."

"I know," Jennifer said. "You could start a true-crime podcast."

I nearly laughed but considering how much true crime had occurred in our little town recently, it wasn't all that farfetched. "I'm hoping the murder rate goes back down to zero. I was thinking more like taking up painting or writing."

Before calling it a day, I always liked to take inventory to make sure we were ready if we happened to get a rush of customers the next day. We were nearly out of lunch items, so I put potatoes on the stove to boil.

By the time I'd assembled several mini shepherd's pies, I was ready for my own dinner. Irma had suggested I stop by the Mermaid Cafe, but I itched to get to the castle to see what else I could learn.

Telling Jennifer I was going for a drive, I grabbed my keys and stepped outside, surprised to see the sun low in the sky. It would be dark by the time I arrived, and I considered putting the visit off until the next morning. I shook off my apprehension and got in the car.

"It's just a house," I told myself. "Just because it looks like an eerie haunted castle, doesn't mean anything." I put the car in reverse and backed out of the driveway. Now that I could see ghosts, they didn't seem so scary. It was the living I had to watch out for.

CHAPTER 9

I turned off from the main road onto the winding street that led to The Amazing Kaslov's home. My headlights shone the way, casting shadows in the woods as I turned left and then right. At one point, a pair of eyes glowed in the beam, and I calmed myself by saying, "It was just a deer. Probably not a tiger or werewolf."

As I calculated the probability of a tiger roaming the woods in northern California, the iron gate loomed ahead. The castle beyond appeared foreboding in the shadows cast by my headlights. I put the car in park, took a deep breath, and got out, leaving the car running and the headlights on.

A tiny sliver of a moon did little to illuminate the dirt road under my feet, so I kept to the area lit by the headlight beam. I pressed the button on the callbox.

No answer.

A noise behind me made me jump, but I managed not to squeal. The woods were full of sounds—

rustling leaves, animals scurrying, and all the other normal forest sounds. My heart pounded and I nearly jumped back into my car, but I really wanted answers.

I softly called, "Theadora. I've come back to talk with you."

A pale face appeared suddenly through the bars of the gate, and this time I did squeal. Thea smiled, appearing to be pleased with herself for startling me.

"Hello again," I said, though it came out as more of a squeak.

"I remember you," she said.

"Yes, nice to see you again. I'm April May. Is your uncle here?"

"Oh, I thought you'd come to talk with me," she said, a note of disappointment in her voice. "You called my name."

"But you're..." Silly me. Of course, Thea was short for Theadora. "I didn't know if your uncle would want me talking with you without him knowing about it."

She pressed her face up against the bars. "I'm an adult, you know. I don't need his permission to talk to people." She pulled back and the bars had left a smudge on her perfect complexion.

"That's great." I was getting tired of talking through the gates, and I hadn't dressed for standing outside. "It's a little chilly out here. Do you think I could come in?"

Thea glanced over her shoulder at the castle then back to me. "Wait here. I'll open the gate."

By the time I got back in my car, the gate was already opening. It closed once I'd entered the grounds.

After I parked and got out, I had the unsettled feeling that I might be walking into a trap.

I shook off my reservations and crossed the little bridge to the front door which stood open. I stepped inside and called out, "Hello?" but no one answered.

The thick carpets muffled my steps as I made my way to the living room. This time, the room felt even colder than it had before, and I soon saw the reason— the fire had gone out. Embers glowed but gave off little heat.

I waited for several minutes, then stuck my head into the kitchen. Martha must have cleaned up from dinner and gone to bed or home. I'd assumed she had a room here with Kaslov and Thea, but that was not necessarily the case.

Growing impatient, I walked down the long hall that led to Kaslov's office. I knocked lightly and pressed my ear up to the door. If anyone were inside, they were being as quiet as a mouse.

I turned the knob, glad to find the door unlocked, and pushed the door open. A quick glance around and I relaxed somewhat. Kaslov must have been busy in another part of the castle, but where was Theadora's ghost? Did she, unlike Chef Emile, have the ability to move around the house? Maybe she could go anywhere she wanted.

It might be fun to be a ghost if you could transport yourself to Paris or the jungles of Africa in the blink of an eye. You could swim with piranhas and not worry about getting eaten alive. Though never getting to taste another cinnamon roll or porterhouse steak would be a drag.

I called out tentatively. "Theadora?"

Papers and notepads covered the top of Kaslov's desk, along with a tape recorder of some sort with a microphone attached. I hadn't seen a Dictaphone for many, many years. Did he have a secretary who typed up his correspondence?

I didn't know that anyone still wrote letters in the age of email, but that's what most of the papers turned out to be—fan mail. Without touching anything, I perused what I could see. Fans gushed over his abilities, his personality, and his handsome looks, perhaps not realizing the reruns they watched were thirty years old. One writer claimed to be his biggest fan, adding that she anxiously awaited his memoir.

That must have been the reason Kaslov had a Dictaphone. He was at the right stage of life to write his life history and still famous enough to get a lucrative publishing contract.

Peeking at his wastebasket, I saw a crumpled, handwritten note. After reading the first line, I stuffed it in my jacket pocket. Was it illegal to steal someone's trash? It was a risk I felt willing to take.

Molina had already conducted a search of the premises, but I wondered how thorough he'd been. Had he missed this piece of evidence if that's what it was? I'd wait until later to decide.

A woman's voice startled me out of my reverie. "You came back."

The transparent figure of the ghost I'd seen the day before hovered a few feet away. I found the sight disconcerting. Chef seemed so much more solid, but maybe ghosts made up their own rules about how to behave.

"Yes." I held my arm over my pocket, hoping she hadn't seen me take the note. "You said Kaslov is in danger. Orson Jennings impersonated him and was killed. If they meant to kill Kaslov, then I agree that he's in danger. I came here to find out what you knew."

"I know he's in danger." Her voice had a thin, melodic quality.

"Yep," I said impatiently. "I think we've established that." Kaslov might enter the room at any minute, and I needed to get information from her, not vague generalities. "Does the danger have to do with Orson's murder?"

She gazed out the window at the grounds outside. "Thea believes she is in love with Orson."

"Well, he's dead now."

"Perhaps that's for the best." She turned back to me, and I felt as if her dark eyes were boring into my soul. "Why did you come back?"

"To talk to you." I broke eye contact with her and shook off the feeling she'd seen inside my soul. No one could do that.

"But why?" She seemed to fade, though it may have been my imagination.

I sighed. "You said Kaslov is in danger, remember? What did you mean?"

Before she answered, the door flung open.

Kaslov glared at me. "What are you doing in my study?"

My mind raced as I decided what to say. I went with my first instinct. "I think you may be in danger." My voice sounded shaky to my ears, reflecting the way I felt after my encounter with Theadora.

He huffed. "That doesn't explain what you're doing here in my study."

"Oh, that." I gave him an apologetic smile. "Thea let me in the gates and left the front door open, but when I entered, I couldn't find her. Or anyone else."

He stared at me for several seconds, then seemed to accept my answer, at least for now. "Have a seat, why don't you?" He took his place behind the desk.

Sitting across from him, my mouth felt dry. He carried himself with an aura of strength and authority which I found intimidating. I waited for him to restart the conversation.

"Why would you think I'm in danger?" he asked. "Here behind the safety of these walls, no one and nothing can reach me unless I want them to."

"Really?" I gestured to myself. "I walked right in."

"Yes, well, I'll have to talk to Thea." He said, a frown of fatherly concern on his face. "She can be much too trusting." He stacked the papers on his desk as if disinterested in our conversation.

"Like with Orson?" I asked, watching carefully for his reaction.

His eyes darted to me. "I don't know what you mean."

"I mean that Thea was, or thought she was, in love

with him. And considering how protective you are, I can't believe you thought the hired help was a suitable match for your niece. On top of that, he was old enough to be her father, wasn't he?"

His cheeks reddened and he spoke through clenched teeth. "You will leave now before I have you thrown out." He stood, adding, "I forbid you to talk to Thea again."

"Theadora spoke to me." I stood and turned to go, adding as I walked to the door. "She's the one who warned me."

"No one calls Thea that," he bellowed.

"I wasn't talking about Thea," I said, as I opened the study door and stepped into the hallway.

As I DROVE down the hill, the castle faded into the darkness in my rearview mirror like a mirage. When I reached the main road, I pulled over, turned on the overhead light, and retrieved the note from my pocket.

Smoothing the wrinkles out as much as I could, I read the uneven scrawl.

Kaslov,

I recommend you improve your offer if you want to get rid of me.

The note wasn't signed, but I had no doubt about who'd written it and why. I folded it and put it back in my pocket planning to show it to Freddie in the morning. Unfortunately, it wouldn't be admissible as evidence if it came to that, but I had no regrets. If I hadn't taken it myself, no one might have ever known that Orson had tried to extort money from Kaslov.

Jennifer left a light on for me. After a few cups of chamomile tea, I climbed the stairs to my room. With so much on my mind, I knew sleep would not come easily.

I lay in bed thinking of the ethereal spirit who'd given me so little information. As much as I'd been frustrated at the time, she may have given me the most important piece of the puzzle: Thea had been in love with Orson. Before I drifted off, I began to wonder if it had anything to do with his death.

THE NEXT MORNING dawned gray and foggy. When I'd first arrived in Serenity Cove earlier that year, I'd learned about May gray and June gloom but what clever rhyme might they have for September? Checking the weather report, I saw that sunshine was expected but not before noon.

I dressed in sweats and made my way downstairs. Without Jennifer greeting me, I felt out of sorts. A quick check of my phone told me she'd sent a late text and spent the night at her grandmother's. I smiled to myself, happy they were getting acquainted and making up for lost time.

Freddie arrived just as the coffee finished brewing, and I warmed up cinnamon muffins for both of us. I put them and a fresh stick of butter on the kitchen island.

When we were settled, I announced, "I went to visit The Amazing Kaslov."

"Alone?"

I nodded. "And I found this." I unfolded the note and laid it in front of her. As she read, I sipped my coffee, feeling my stomach tighten as I waited for her reprimand. I didn't have to wait long.

"What do you mean you found this?" The tone of her voice expressed disbelief. "Where?"

I gave her my best "don't be mad at me" smile. "In Kaslov's trash can."

"April!" She closed her eyes and took a few breaths to calm herself. "You know this is now inadmissible as evidence."

"I know," I said, now on the defensive. "But how admissible would it have been rotting away at the county dump? Molina already searched Kaslov's home, and he wouldn't have any reason to go back a second time."

"You don't know that." Freddie's stern voice scolded.

"Look. Molina missed this the first time. Was there an infinitesimal chance that he'd find it? Maybe. But this is a big clue."

"Why would Kaslov give Orson money?" Freddie asked. "It makes no sense."

"It does once you know that Thea was in love with Orson."

Freddie's mouth dropped open. "But she's not much more than a teenager. And he's... he's..."

"Old," I said, finishing her sentence. "I know. Kaslov refused to talk about it."

~

JENNIFER ARRIVED in time to help me get ready for the day. The tearoom was fairly busy for a Thursday, and I appreciated having the distraction from all my thoughts of murder. When the last guest left and we'd cleaned up, I invited Jennifer to go with me to the Mermaid Café for dinner.

"I think I'll stay home if that's okay with you," she said. "I feel like I need an evening to myself. I love spending time with my family, but..."

"But sometimes you need a break," I said, completing her sentence.

"Exactly. You don't mind, do you?"

I chuckled at her puppy dog expression. "Of course not. Enjoy your evening." I had a feeling she'd spend it with Jane Austin, either reading or watching a movie based on one of her books.

Soon, I stepped inside the otherworldly Mermaid Cafe, with its undulating lights in shades of aqua and violet. When my eyes adjusted to the dim light, I spotted Freddie and Angeline at the bar. Angeline spoke to a woman with wavy brown hair, and as I came closer, I recognized Sarah.

"April," Angeline said, standing to give me a hug. "We were just talking about you."

"You were?" I wasn't sure I liked the sound of that.

Sarah laughed at my obvious discomfort. "Freddie

was just bragging about your cooking. I'd love to get your quiche recipe, that is if you don't mind sharing it."

"Not at all," I said. "As long as you share your recipe for cinnamon rolls."

"Gladly, but they take forever to make." She proceeded to give me a quick list of all the steps involved.

"I think I'll leave the cinnamon roll baking to you," I said. "I prefer simpler recipes whenever I can help it."

"I'll give you my recipe for cinnamon muffins then. They're almost as delicious and not nearly as much work."

Irma finished serving a patron at the other end of the bar and came over to take my order. "What will you have?"

"I'm not sure," I said. "A mixed drink. Something sweet but not too sweet."

"A Storm Warning, coming right up." She filled a tall glass with ice. As she added rum and ginger ale and added a squeeze of lime, a ray of light shone across her face as the door opened behind me. She glanced up to see who'd entered and scowled. "Son of a bucket."

I turned around to see who had arrived. Deputy Molina walked straight for us, with the young deputy I'd seen on the day of the murder close behind him.

He greeted each of us, then said, "This is not a social call, I'm afraid. I have an arrest to make."

Freddie jumped off her stool. "No! You can't arrest her. She wouldn't hurt a fly."

Angeline laid a hand on her arm. "Calm down, dear."

Molina glared at Freddie. "Stay out of this."

"But—"

Molina held up a hand to stop her from saying anything else.

"Sarah Arvin," he said. "I'm placing you under arrest for the murder of Orson Jennings."

CHAPTER 10

*W*e sat in stunned silence for several moments and then all started talking at once. Molina ignored our questions and took Sarah by the arm, leading her to the door.

I turned to Freddie. "We need to find out what evidence he has."

She stared at the door as it swung closed. "I think I have a pretty good idea."

Angeline nudged her daughter. "And?"

Freddie sighed. "The knife had been wiped clean of fingerprints. All but one. Before Molina shut me out of the investigation, he told me he'd run the print, but it wasn't in AFIS."

"AFIS?" I asked.

"Automated Fingerprint Identification System. It's the database for criminal data including fingerprints. When he didn't get a match, he fingerprinted everyone who was at the event that day."

"You think that was Sarah's fingerprint on the knife?" Angeline asked. "She stabbed Orson?"

Irma folded her arms over her chest. "I don't believe that for a minute."

I'd considered Sarah's husband a possible suspect, but never her. "Why would she kill Orson? Or Kaslov, assuming he was the intended victim?"

Freddie took a deep breath in and out before answering. "Hopefully she doesn't have a motive."

I brightened. "If she doesn't have a motive, they can't convict her, right?"

Freddie gave me a look normally reserved for naive children. "It might make it harder to convict her, but a motive isn't necessary for conviction."

I felt my spirit deflate. "Poor Sarah."

Freddie stepped outside to make a call, and when she returned, she gave Angeline her car keys and asked me if we could talk somewhere. I didn't want to stay and eat dinner after what had happened, so I said goodbye to Angeline and Irma and followed Freddie outside. The sun had dipped below the horizon and the sky, streaked with pink clouds, reflected on the calm ocean waters.

I suggested we go to my home and Freddie agreed. We said little as we hurried along through the chilly evening air.

While I made a pot of tea and fixed us a snack of toasted baguette slices with cream cheese and salmon, Freddie started the fire. Her phone rang, and I overheard her speak briefly to someone, but I didn't catch the words.

I carried everything to the coffee table in front of the fireplace and poured her a cup of spiced herbal tea that I'd found to be both calming and invigorating. Knowing she'd have mixed feelings over the turn of events, I waited for her to bring up the subject.

She finally spoke, her voice soft and tentative. "I nearly panicked when Deputy Molina said he was making an arrest. I was so sure he'd come for my mother."

"I was afraid of that too. You must have been so relieved when you realized it wasn't Angeline he'd come to arrest."

She sighed. "Relieved and shocked. I never in a million years would have thought that Sarah was capable of something like that."

"You actually think she murdered Orson?" I felt stunned that she'd believe such a thing.

"That was Molina on the phone," Freddie explained. "He confirmed that Sarah's fingerprint was on the murder weapon. How would Sarah's fingerprint end up on the blade of the knife if she didn't stab Orson with it?"

That was a good question, but I felt sure there was an answer that made more sense than a pink-loving, muffin-baking innkeeper being a murderer. I took a long sip of the fragrant tea, the spices reminding me of mulled cider. I shook off my longing to forget all the worries of the day and told myself to focus. Why *would* Sarah's fingerprint be on the...?

"Did you say blade?" I asked.

She tilted her head to one side, probably wondering

why I'd asked, then answered. "Yes."

I got up and went to the kitchen, returning with a steak knife, handing it to Freddie, handle first. As expected, she gave me a questioning look.

"Hold that knife like you're going to stab me," I instructed.

Freddie gripped the handle and thrust it in my direction. "Or I might stab you underhand, like this." She changed her grip and held the knife by her side. "But based on the location of the wound, I'd say whoever stabbed Orson, did it overhand." She changed her grip and demonstrated again.

"Now take a look at the knife," I said, and when she held the knife, I knew she'd come to the same realization I had.

"I never touched the blade," she said. "Why would Sarah put her fingers on the blade?"

"Now hold the knife by the blade. Be careful." When she did as I'd asked, I took a napkin and began wiping off the handle. As I did, I touched the blade with my other hand to steady it.

Freddie's eyes widened. "Sarah wiped the fingerprints off the knife." She frowned as another thought occurred to her. "That doesn't mean she didn't kill him in a fit of passion, then wipe the handle."

"True, but it also means that someone else might have killed Orson and Sarah wanted to protect him."

"Him?" Freddie asked.

There was only one person Sarah would want to protect. "Her husband Simon."

I told Freddie about the flirting I'd witnessed

between Sarah and the man we'd thought was The Amazing Kaslov. "Orson seemed to be the instigator, but Sarah appeared to be enjoying the attention."

Freddie smirked. "If you were married to Simon, wouldn't you appreciate getting some attention?" She shrugged one shoulder. "He seems like a nice man, but I can't see him showering Sarah with sweet nothings, can you?"

I thought back to when I'd last seen them together. "He's not big with the words."

Part of me thought that if Sarah had tried to cover up the murder to protect her husband that she deserved to go to jail, but then I wasn't sure what I would do in her situation. How far would I go to protect someone I loved?

On the other hand, if Simon had killed Orson, he deserved to be locked up for the rest of his life. The problem was, I couldn't convince myself that Simon had done it.

"You think Simon could get angry enough to kill someone?" I asked Freddie.

She stared into the fire, lost in thought.

"Freddie?"

"Huh?" She turned to face me, a sad look on her face. "Sorry. I'm just having a moment. I asked myself if I'd let Sarah go to jail if it meant keeping my mother safe, and I didn't like the answer." She stared at her hands folded in her lap. "When I became a doctor, I pledged to dedicate my life to the service of humanity. I've always believed in truth and justice. What happened to me?"

I reached out and patted her arm. "What happened is your instinct to protect your mother overrode your better judgment. That's completely natural. You and I know you're better than that. And we know that Angeline didn't kill anyone. I don't think Sarah did either, but until we know the truth, I don't think either one of us can let it go."

She gave me a weak smile. "I know you can't. Nobody is getting away with murder in this town as long as you're around."

"Not as long as I have you to help me catch them."

Freddie and I agreed we needed to talk to Sarah. I called Deputy Molina to ask about visiting hours, and after explaining that I was a friend of Sarah's he relented. "You can see her tomorrow. After nine."

"Let's go see Simon." I stood and threw my purse over my shoulder.

"Now?" Freddie didn't move from her seat. "He just found out his wife was arrested. He's probably at the station right now trying to see her and arrange counsel. If she's covering for him, then maybe he'll confess, and it'll all be over with."

I sighed. "I suppose you're right."

"I'll be at the clinic all day tomorrow, but I'll call Molina and find out what charges he's filing. Depending on what time the bail hearing is, maybe Irma can go with you in the morning to see Sarah. I'm sure that would cheer her up." She stood to go. "I'll message you as soon as I know more."

I hated to think of poor Sarah in a jail cell overnight, but there was little I could do. If they let

Simon visit her tonight, and if he did kill Orson, I hoped he would do the right thing and turn himself in.

I WOKE before dawn and stared at my phone waiting for Freddie's message. I'd just gotten dressed when it came, telling me that Sarah would be transferred to county jail later that morning for her arraignment, and I'd better get to the police station soon if I wanted to see her.

Irma didn't answer the phone or respond to my texts, so I swung by her house. I knocked and waited, then knocked again.

Irma came to the door and greeted me with, "What are you doing here at this time of the morning?"

After I explained we needed to make an early start if we wanted to be able to see Sarah, Irma said she couldn't go with me.

"Why not?" I asked, surprised that she didn't want to go along.

"I have a doctor's appointment," she said, then closed the door in my face.

"Was it something I said?" I asked the door, which didn't answer. "Fine. I'll go by myself."

There wasn't any time to call anyone else to go with me, and besides, there wasn't anyone other than Irma I would want by my side. Confused by her behavior, I got in the car and drove to the police station, calling Freddie from the car.

"Where are you?" Freddie asked. "You sound like you're driving. You better be using hands-free."

"Yes, of course, I am," I answered. "I'm on my way to the police station. Irma said she's seeing a doctor this morning. Is her appointment with you?"

"She has a doctor's appointment?" Freddie sounded surprised.

I pulled into the parking lot next to the building shared by city hall and the police station. "I'm here. I'll call you back after I talk to Sarah *if* I even get to see her."

I hung up before Freddie replied. I thought Sarah was important to Irma and Freddie, and I felt like Sarah and I were both being abandoned. I got out of the car and gave myself a quick pep talk. "Sarah needs a friend right now, and it looks like I'm it."

Pushing my shoulders back, I pulled open the heavy door and headed down the hallway to Molina's office. I stepped inside the door, prepared to demand to see Sarah right away.

Someone else sat at Molina's desk.

The broad-shouldered man in his tan sheriff's uniform and tie had to be at least a decade older than Molina. Maybe two. His sandy-blonde hair was flecked with gray and the deep lines on his face along with a scar next to one eye told me he'd done a lot of living in his time on earth. He had the rugged good looks of an aging action star.

I knew I was gawking, but I didn't care. "Who are you?"

CHAPTER 11

*T*he man rose from his chair, and he must have stood six foot four at least. "I'm Sheriff Anderson Fontana. And you are?" He kept his deep voice neutral giving the impression of a man in complete control of his emotions.

"I'm April May, I run the SereniTea tearoom here in town. You're *the* sheriff? Deputy Molina's boss?"

He gave me a curt nod. "Deputy Molina has been reassigned. Would you care to take a seat, Ms. May?" he asked, gesturing to the chairs in front of his desk.

"I'd love to chat, but I need to talk to Sarah before she gets transferred."

He gave me a friendly smile, which I found unsettling. "Please, just a moment of your time. I'll make sure you get to see her."

I hesitated, but since I had a feeling I wouldn't get to see Sarah without his permission, I took a seat on one of the hard plastic chairs facing his desk.

"This is the second murder in your place of business, is that correct?" he asked, still smiling.

Not sure why he would smile while talking about murder, I nodded and waited to see what other questions he might have.

"And there have been other murders since your relatively recent arrival in town."

I felt my mouth open in disbelief, then shut it. Was he implying that I was involved somehow? "Yes," I said, then mirrored his smile and added, "One of them was committed by the former acting police chief."

His smile faded. "Yes, a most unfortunate incident. Deputy Molina insisted you had nothing to do with any of the deaths, but you can see how it looks, can't you? I've reviewed all the case files, and it appears he was right."

"Of course, he was," I sniped. I didn't add that I had helped solve the first three murders, and I would help solve this one if I had to. "Don't think I haven't wondered once or twice if I'd made the right choice settling down here. But most of the people in Serenity Cove are wonderful. The fact that there have been several murders since I moved here is purely coincidental. I mean, not the first one, since the Police Chief and my realtor were trying to steal jewels hidden in my house. But the others had nothing to do with me."

The smile returned to his face crinkling the corners of his eyes. I'd heard that if a smile reached your eyes that it was genuine. I'd also heard, knowing that, a genuine smile could be faked.

"I apologize for my bluntness. In my line of work,

it's usually an asset, but please know I didn't mean to offend you. I've been told that you know most of the people involved in this case, and I hoped you could help me complete my notes."

That sounded promising. "I've gotten to know half the town by now I think, and I can tell you that Sarah didn't murder anyone."

He sighed. "That's one of the reasons I took over the case. The arrest may have been rushed."

His words gave me a jolt of hope. "Yes," I agreed. "I think it was." Finally, someone who didn't jump to conclusions. "Not to say that Deputy Molina isn't competent," I quickly added. "He just doesn't have the experience and knowledge that might be required for a murder investigation."

"It sounds like you were fond of him," he said.

I nodded, remembering how much Molina frustrated me at times. "You might say I feel about him like a son who never takes my advice. I give very good advice, by the way."

"I'll keep that in mind." Sheriff Fontana shuffled some papers on his desk, picked up one, silently reading it before speaking. "The arrest report states that there was a fingerprint on the murder weapon that was identified to be that of Mrs. Sarah Arvin."

"On the blade," I said. "Who would hold the blade of a knife if they were going to stab someone? You'd hold the handle." His eyebrows raised slightly, and I wondered if I'd said too much. I shrugged. "You can't keep anything secret in this town."

He shuffled a few more papers and seemed to find what he was looking for.

"So," he began as he perused the page. He looked up and made eye contact, which he held as he spoke. "What is your theory as to why the suspect's fingerprint is on the knife?"

I paused, not sure how much to say until I talked to Sarah, but I folded under his steady gaze. "She might be covering for someone. I think she accidentally got her fingerprint on the blade while wiping prints off the handle."

"I see." He seemed to think over my idea. "That's not a bad theory. And do you know who she might be covering for?"

I sank back in my chair. It was one thing to talk among my friends about who might have murdered Orson Jennings, but to give the sheriff a name when I had no proof?

"It's complete conjecture on my part," I said.

He arranged the papers on his desk into a stack and then shoved them into a file before returning his attention to me. "Off the record."

"It's just a wild guess. I don't think it would be appropriate for me to accuse someone of murder with no more than a hunch."

"I understand." His expression shifted and he stared at the wall for a moment, as if a sad memory had intruded on his thoughts. "Ms. May," he began.

"You can call me April."

"April," he said, the smile returning to his face. "I'm pretty sure I want the same thing as you, at least as it pertains to this case. Justice. I put bad guys—and gals—behind bars. I have no interest in locking up innocent people. I promise you I won't arrest anyone based on your hunch."

I chuckled. "No, of course, you wouldn't." Taking another look at Sheriff Fontana, with his strong jawline and wide shoulders, I felt reassured. Finally, we had an officer with experience, intelligence, and integrity. The real murderer would be behind bars in no time.

"It's just a theory, remember, but I think she might be covering for her husband, Simon."

AFTER SHERIFF FONTANA checked my I.D. and temporarily confiscated my purse and phone, he led me to a cell where I'd once spent a few long hours. I hated to think of how hard it must have been for Sarah to spend the entire night locked up in the tiny room.

Fontana unlocked the door and held it open for me. "I'll be back in fifteen minutes."

Sarah jumped up from the bed where she'd been sitting and rushed to hug me. "Thank you for coming."

Her smile didn't fool me. Her lashes were damp from tears and her nose red. For all I knew she'd spent the entire night crying.

"Did you get any sleep?" I asked.

Her eyes darted to the bed. "A little. Mostly I read. Simon brought me a few books and magazines."

"I'm so sorry this is happening. I'm sure it's all a big

mistake and you'll be home at the B&B in no time. You just need to stay positive, okay?"

She said nothing as emotions seemed to get the better of her. She did her best to smile as she blinked back tears.

"Sarah, I don't have much time and I really need to ask you something," I began.

Her brown eyes widened. "What is it?"

"Who…" I began but struggled to get the words out. I took a deep breath and tried again. "Who are you trying to protect?"

She looked away and walked back to the bed. She sat down before responding. "What do you mean?"

I crossed my arms over my chest as I watched her. "I know you didn't kill Kaslov. But you wiped the knife handle clean."

She lowered her chin and stared at her hands. "You're wrong. I did kill him."

I felt my frustration build. "I hope you didn't tell Molina or the sheriff that." When she didn't answer, I went on to explain. "Here's what's going to happen if you confess to Kaslov's murder. You're going to be held for a long time while they try to put together a case. At some point, they'll realize you didn't do it and realize you're covering for someone. It will be a very short leap from you to Simon."

Her eyes shot up. I had her full attention now.

"All you're doing is delaying the inevitable," I continued. "What we need to do now is be proactive. Hopefully, the sheriff will find the real murderer soon, but Freddie and I are doing our own investigation. Do you have a lawyer?"

"They said I can get a public defender when... if they charge me. After the arraignment. I think that's going to be today."

"You need a lawyer now." I wanted her to have someone by her side who would keep her from confessing to a murder she didn't commit.

She hung her head, and mumbled, "I can't afford one."

"I can." Before she could object, I added, "You need to be home with your husband baking muffins and fluffing pillows. In the meantime, don't say anything to Sheriff Fontana until the attorney arrives. Not a word, do you understand?"

She nodded and mimicked zipping her lips and throwing the key away. A small smile of hope played on her lips.

BACK IN MY CAR, I called my attorney and he promised to arrange for a defense attorney to meet with Sarah. Next, I drove straight to the Serenity Cove B&B, parked, and climbed up the painted wooden steps to the front door of the converted Victorian home. Normally, I'd walk right in, but nothing about this week was normal, so I knocked gently then entered.

The lobby felt deserted as I moved through it to the dining area. A jolt of fear stabbed at me. Simon might be here alone. Simon, who could be a murderer.

As I was about to give up and leave, I found Simon slumped in a chair at one of the tables. From what I could tell, he hadn't noticed my arrival. He stared at a muffin on a plate in front of him, untouched.

I cleared my throat, hoping not to startle him, and spoke gently. "Hello, Simon."

He looked up and blinked, not appearing to recognize me at first.

"It's me, April. From the tearoom."

"Oh." His gaze returned to the muffin.

"I just went to see Sarah. She seems to be in good spirits, considering." He said nothing, so I kept talking. "You were able to see her for a few minutes last night, weren't you?"

He nodded.

My frustration grew at this man who appeared uninterested in doing anything to get his wife out of jail. "I understand they're transferring her to the county courthouse for her bail hearing. Why didn't you go see her this morning?"

"She told me not to." He glanced at me with sad eyes then stared at the empty buffet.

"But you'll be going to her bail hearing later, of course." Again, no answer. "Won't you?"

"Can't."

My anger began to rise, which was never a good thing. "Can't? Or won't? What is wrong with you. Your wife is in jail all because of you, and you sit here like a bump on a log. Why aren't you at least trying to do something?"

He blinked back the tears but a few escaped before

he pulled a handkerchief out of his pocket to blow his nose. "You said, 'because of me.'"

"Yes." My anger faded slightly at the sight of his tears. "Don't you know? She thinks you killed Orson in a jealous rage and now she's covering for you." The moment I said the words, I realized how ridiculous they were. This man might be upset or heartbroken if he thought another man coveted his wife, but I couldn't imagine him in a fit of rage. "But you didn't kill him, did you?"

He shook his head and spoke in barely more than a whisper. "My poor, sweet Sarah."

"You need to talk to her as soon as possible and tell her that you didn't kill Orson. Then she can tell her attorney everything and they can get the charges dropped."

He stood, a look of determination on his face I hadn't seen before. "I'll do it right now."

I nearly jumped when I heard footsteps coming up behind me. I turned to see Sheriff Fontana standing in the dining room doorway.

"Ms. May. How nice to see you again," he said, as if on a social call. "I hope you didn't come here to warn Mr. Arvin."

"Warn him?" I asked. "Warn him of what?"

His eyes went from me to Simon. "Simon Arvin, you're under arrest."

CHAPTER 12

*A*s I drove home, I gave myself a talking to. I'd wanted to help, but the only thing my meddling had accomplished was getting Simon thrown in jail. And we hadn't even gotten Sarah out yet. Would she be charged as an accomplice?

I still had trouble accepting that quiet, mild-mannered Simon could be a killer. But wasn't that what people said when they found out a serial killer had been living in their neighborhood? "He seemed like such a nice man—always kept to himself."

As I pulled into my driveway, a quick glance at my watch threw me into a panic. My tearoom opened in ten minutes! I burst through the back door, then into the kitchen where I found Jennifer looking surprisingly calm. Savory aromas filled the air, mixing with the smell of freshly baked shortbread. A tray of scones sat on the counter ready to pop into the oven.

Irma sat at the island, munching on cookies. "It's

about time you got here. Poor Jennifer's been working her tail off."

I smacked Irma playfully on the arm before giving Jennifer a hug. "I'm so sorry to leave you to do everything by yourself."

She grinned. "You've trained me well. Besides, you do such a good job of prepping everything, it hardly took any time at all."

I grinned. "I have the best assistant."

"And I have the best boss," Jennifer added.

"Okay, enough of this love fest," Irma grouched. "She's wonderful, you're wonderful, now can we get on with our lives?"

Jennifer ignored Irma. "We don't open for a few minutes, and I've got everything ready to go." She gestured to a stool. "Why don't you sit down and have a cup of tea and tell us about Sarah. Is she okay?"

I sighed. "I hired a lawyer for her, but outside of that one good deed, I think I made everything worse." I told them about meeting Sheriff Fontana and my visits with Sarah and Simon. "It might have been my fault that Simon got arrested too. Probably was."

Irma shook her head. "It's Sarah's own fault. If she wiped off the knife, that was a pretty dumb thing to do."

"True," I said. "But she thought she was protecting her husband. I don't like to think of her spending time in county jail. The most she should be charged with is obstruction of justice I would think. Hopefully we'll hear something soon."

Irma grabbed another shortbread cookie. "If Simon

is charged with murder, then wouldn't Sarah be an accessory?"

I sighed. "I don't know. I sure hope not—that sounds bad."

Jennifer glanced at the clock. "It's almost noon. I'll go unlock the front door."

I remembered the reason Irma had given me for not going with me to see Sarah. "How was the doctor's visit. Everything okay?"

Jennifer stopped in the doorway and turned back. "What's wrong?"

"Nothing's wrong," Irma said with a scowl. "This is why I don't tell you people things. You're always fussing over me." She grabbed her jacket and walking stick and slipped out the back door before either one of us could say another word.

Luckily the tearoom didn't have many visitors all day. That wouldn't be my normal attitude about a slow business day, but with all the other things on my mind like Sarah and Simon's arrests, I found it hard to focus on baking or making tea sandwiches.

Freddie called to tell me they had charged Sarah with obstruction of justice instead of first-degree murder and let her out on her own recognizance. Simon's bail wouldn't be set until the following day.

When the last customer left, Jennifer finished cleaning up while I browned chopped onions and garlic.

"That smells so good," she said. "What are you making?"

I held up a parsnip. "More parsnip and carrot soup. I found more parsnips on the front porch."

"More?" she asked. "Is that the same person who left the beets the other day?"

"I guess so. Unless more than one person is giving us their extra produce. I thought it came out great and it's so easy. Customers seemed to like it too."

I poured two bowls of soup for Jennifer and me, and we carried them to one of the tables in the front room. We'd just sat down to eat when Freddie's voice came from the kitchen.

"We're in the front room," I called back.

Freddie emerged through the kitchen door and came over to our table. "What happened today?" she asked, giving me a scolding look. "You were just supposed to talk to Sarah, not get Simon arrested."

I cringed at her accusation. "I didn't do it on purpose." For the second time, I recounted my day, filling her in on the details of everything that had happened. "Did you know Molina was getting reassigned?"

Freddie took a seat across from us. "Not until an hour ago. The sheriff called me in to have a meeting with him. He asked about my relationship with you."

I raised an eyebrow. "And what did you tell him?"

"I told him that Serenity Cove is a tiny town and I'm friends with a number of the residents. Then he said, yeah, especially people who are involved with multiple murders."

I gasped. "He said that?"

"Or words to that effect. He also gloated that he'd

solved the murder in just a few hours. I think he meant to imply that Molina and I are incompetent."

"Did he really?" My feelings for Fontana changed from admiration to aversion, and I wished he'd go back to wherever he came from. "What a jerk. Molina may have been inexperienced, but at least he didn't go around arresting people without solid evidence. Well, except for Sarah, but I'm sure he would have let her go pretty quickly. And Fontana better not insult you to my face or he's going to get an earful."

Freddie tried but failed to hide her smile. "Do me a favor. Just stay away from him. It's best if you stay off his radar, especially if the D.A. decides not to charge Simon and Sarah."

"Why especially?" I asked. "Wouldn't it be a good thing if the charges are dropped?"

"Yes, but then he might turn his attention to my mother. Between her argument with the victim and the earring—"

Jennifer, who'd been quiet up till now, asked, "What earring?"

"The less you know the better," Freddie said.

I finished my soup and offered Freddie a bowl, but she declined. I carried the empty bowls to the kitchen, returning with a notepad. "We need to solve this murder and fast. I think it's time for a new list of suspects."

"Why fast?" Jennifer said. "I mean, I know you want to get Simon released from jail, but as long as everyone thinks he's the murderer, maybe the real one will let their guard down."

"Jennifer!" I looked at my assistant with admiration. "That's a great insight."

She blushed. "I've learned about more than just baking since I've met you."

"And you've got a good point," Freddie said. "But I think April's worried because when someone resorts to murder, that means they've crossed over a line. And they don't always stop with one."

"Oh." Jennifer leaned back in her seat, the seriousness of the situation sinking in.

The notepad already had a list of suspects we'd made days earlier. I read off the names. "Angeline," I began. "Freddie made me write that," I explained to Jennifer. "Next, Harriet, Sarah, and Simon." I turned the paper over, but there were no more names. "Is that it?"

"Remember the note," Freddie said, and I added Kaslov's name to the list.

"What note?" Jennifer asked.

Freddie's eyes met mine before she answered. "The less you know about that too, the better."

"I don't like knowing less," Jennifer complained. "I want to know more. Why are you keeping things from me?"

I patted her on the arm. "I understand. But if Molina questions you again, wouldn't you rather not have information that could implicate Angeline?"

Her eyes widened.

"And April," Freddie added.

"All you need to know," I explained, "Is that Angeline didn't kill anyone, but Kaslov may have. It turns out he had a motive to kill Orson, but I obtained that information in a sketchy way. That's why we're keeping it from you. To protect you."

Jennifer didn't seem convinced, but she didn't ask any more questions.

Freddie's phone buzzed. She stood and said Angeline had dinner waiting for her at home. I followed her to the back door.

"You think the murderer will try to kill again?" I asked as she stepped outside.

"There's no way to know for sure, but I'm not going to feel safe until the right person is behind bars."

JENNIFER and I spent the morning prepping for the day. Fridays tended to be busier than the other weekdays, though not as busy as the weekend. I began to seriously consider cutting back our hours at least until things picked up in the spring. We had a few regulars who stopped by for lunch during the week, but I wasn't sure it justified staying open six days a week.

While Jennifer made a run to the store for some fresh fruit and vegetables, I took a break. I turned the kettle on and chatted with Emile, who seemed focused on his writing.

"Another cookbook?" I asked.

He shook his head but otherwise ignored me.

"Your memoirs?" This time he didn't react. "That's it, isn't it? You're writing your life story. That's wonderful! Maybe one of these days you could read it to me. I'd love to know more about your life."

"Hmph," he grunted.

"Fine. I can take a hint." I scooped my favorite rose tea into the teapot's infuser and poured the hot, not boiling, water in.

A few minutes later, I poured myself a cup and sat at the island with the suspect list I'd made the night before. I drew a horizontal line under the existing names and wrote down everyone I could remember being at the psychic fair. Those I didn't have names for, I wrote a brief description.

Then I checked off those I'd seen outside when I put out the trash can fire. Assuming the murder happened during the diversion, which seemed a good assumption, then they could be eliminated as possible suspects. Mr. Featherman and the other vendors had stayed inside, but they could vouch for each other's whereabouts.

A "bloop" noise came from somewhere around the sink and I looked up to see if I'd left the faucet on. I stared, waiting for the next drop, but the moment I looked away, I heard another "bloop." This time I watched until I heard the sound again, but I couldn't identify the source of the sound.

"Well, that's going to drive me nuts. Did you hear that?" I asked Emile. "That blooping sound?"

He appeared annoyed with my interruption as if he didn't have all the time in the world to write his memoirs.

The noise bugged me, and I wouldn't be able to

ignore it until I found the source. "It sounds like it's coming from the pipes, doesn't it?"

Emile stared up at the ceiling for a moment, then looked into my eyes. I'd never seen such depth of feeling in his expression. I held my breath as I waited to hear what he had to say.

He took a deep breath and let it out slowly, prolonging the anticipation. "I am a chef, *ma cherie*, not a plumber."

CHAPTER 13

*T*here was only one person I wanted working on my house, but Mark had made it clear that he would get in touch when he returned from his so-called vacation. After what had happened with his last girlfriend, he needed some time alone to reflect and recover. I couldn't imagine how mixed up his feelings must have been—grief, anger, and who knew what other emotions. How does anyone recover from that?

Still, I needed a plumber, and I told myself Mark wouldn't want me hiring someone without asking him first. I sent him a text asking for a recommendation.

When Jennifer returned from her shopping errand, I forgot about the plumbing. We had a good turnout for lunch, and the Crime Scene Cake turned out to be very popular.

The back door opened as I assembled cucumber sandwiches for our first afternoon tea guests of the day. I turned around expecting Irma or Freddie, but instead, Mark stood in the kitchen doorway.

The sight of him made me catch my breath. Dressed as usual in jeans and a work shirt, with a tool belt slung around his slim hips, he seemed so comfortable in his own skin. His smile made the corners of his dark eyes crinkle.

Without thinking, I ran over to him and threw my arms around him. He might not have been expecting a hug, but his strong arms wrapped around me squeezing gently but firmly.

We pulled back from the embrace but held onto each other's hands for several more moments.

"You look great," I finally said as I reluctantly let go of his hands.

"You too." His smile appeared genuine, and I hoped it meant he had begun to heal from his ordeal. "So, about that plumbing issue?"

"Oh, right," I said, remembering why he'd come. "It's just a noise that I heard coming from the sink. It might be nothing."

"But it might be something. I'll take a look."

Jennifer came into the kitchen. "The tray's not ready yet?" She noticed Mark's presence and squealed.

They hugged and chatted for a moment while I finished the tray, then Jennifer carried it into the tearoom. My heart felt light as I watched Mark crawl under the sink, happy to have him back in my life.

After a trip to his truck, he announced the problem was fixed. "Good thing you noticed the sound before it got worse and flooded the whole kitchen."

"Good thing you were available." I decided not to ask about his vacation or say anything to remind him about why he'd taken the break from work. He gave me another hug, briefer this time.

"We should go out for coffee or a drink sometime," he said. Before I answered, he slipped out the back door.

Jennifer came into the kitchen and looked around. "Is Mark gone?"

"For now," I said. "But he'll be back."

JENNIFER and I were in the middle of an afternoon rush, and I'd returned to the kitchen after serving a tiered tray full of sandwiches, scones, and sweets when I found Irma in my kitchen. She stood next to the island with her hands on her hips. "Didn't you see my texts?" she asked.

The phone rang and since it was Freddie's name on the screen, I answered, holding up one finger to suggest that Irma wait a moment. My suggestion obviously annoyed her greatly.

"The District Attorney has decided not to charge Simon in Orson's murder," she said.

"What does that mean?" I asked. "Is he free?"

Irma frowned while Freddie told me the details. Sheriff Fontana could arrest anyone as long as he had probable cause, but it was up to the D.A. to decide if there was enough evidence to prosecute.

As soon as I hung up the phone, Irma groused, "I wanted to be the one to tell you." She took a seat at the island and put her chin in her hands.

"Sorry." I handed her a plate of cookies to make it up to her. "But maybe you can tell me if Sarah and Simon are really in the clear. Could the D.A. change his mind later if he found more evidence?"

Irma shrugged. "I suppose so."

Jennifer poked her head in the kitchen and said, "Another afternoon tea for two, please," before slipping back into the tearoom.

"Where are the scones?" I asked myself. I'd forgotten to bake another batch. Luckily, I'd turned the oven on, and the scones were on a cookie sheet ready to go, so they'd be ready in ten minutes. "My mind is a jumbled mess."

"It's no wonder," Irma said. "Running a tearoom is a full-time job. Add to that solving a murder, and it's a lot. Which reminds me, I have a restaurant to run." She stood and pointed to my phone. "It looks like you missed a call."

I said goodbye to Irma and listened to Kaslov's voice on my voicemail.

"There are many things I have told no one. There is one secret I must divulge before I die—"

The message cut off. I called the number and listened as it rang and rang. A few minutes later, I hit redial, but again, no one answered. By the fifth time, I gave up.

When the last customer left and we'd cleaned up, I told Jennifer my plans to go to the Mermaid Cafe to see Irma. I left out the part about asking her to go with me to the castle to see Kaslov.

The sun wouldn't set for at least an hour, but a chill

had already set in the air. I pulled my coat tighter and hurried along the sidewalk that bordered the beach. A few brave surfers lingered in the water hoping to get one more great ride. As I passed the pier, seagulls swooped over the few remaining anglers with their rods and buckets.

When I entered the Mermaid Cafe, I looked around for Irma but didn't spot her. A young man tended the bar, and when I asked for her, he shrugged and told me she hadn't come in that day. I'd never known Irma to take a day off.

"Diane's in charge if you want to talk to her," he said.

I thanked him and left. After a moment of indecision, I went home for my car and drove to Irma's.

Her lawn needed mowing, and the shrubs on either side of the steps could use a good trimming. I knocked on the door and waited. After double-checking that her car was in her driveway, I knocked again, harder.

The door opened slowly, and her glare greeted me. She wore a pair of Snoopy pajamas and matching slippers.

"Are you sick?" I asked. Only after the words came out did it occur to me that my question might have sounded rude. Then I reminded myself this was Irma I was talking to.

"Go away," she grumbled, then closed the door.

I pushed it open and followed her to the living room. "What's wrong? You never miss work."

She sat in her recliner and pushed it back until her legs were elevated. Staring at the TV, which showed zombies chasing someone through a bleak landscape, I thought she might be planning to ignore me until I went away.

If there was one person more stubborn than Irma, it was me. "Talk to me, Irma."

Still gazing at the TV, she said, "I'm dying."

I laughed. "You'll never die. You're too stubborn." When her expression didn't change, I felt my chest tighten. "You're serious."

"As a heart attack." She grimaced. "Unfortunate choice of words."

"You had a heart attack? Why didn't you tell me?"

She tore her gaze away from the on-screen apocalypse and looked me in the eye. "I don't want anyone feeling sorry for me." She waved a threatening finger at me. "If you tell anyone, it will be the last thing you say."

"Oh... okay." That explained the doctor's visit the previous day. "What did the doctor say?"

"You know how they are. Signed me up for a battery of tests. But I see the way they look at me, that look of pity. They think I can't handle the truth."

"I know it's scary, Irma." Vague platitudes were all that came to mind, any of which might cause Irma to bite my head off. "I'm here for you, you know. Whatever you need."

"I'm not scared of dying," Irma said. "I just hadn't gotten around to doing everything I wanted to do." She tilted her head as she regarded me. "Are you afraid of dying?"

The question caught me off guard. Most likely, I had many years to live, but no one had a guarantee.

I took a seat on the sofa. "I was hospitalized once while on a business trip and had to have emergency surgery in the middle of the night. It wasn't risky or anything, but I couldn't help thinking that I might die, and I had no one to call, no one to be with me. I don't think I'm afraid of dying, although I'd rather live to a hundred as long as I'm reasonably healthy and fit. But I would hate to die alone."

Irma's hand reached for mine and we sat there for a minute or two holding hands, not saying a word.

When Irma yanked her hand away, she asked, "What are you doing here anyway?"

I thought about telling Irma about Kaslov's message, but she had other things to worry about. "I stopped by the Mermaid Cafe and when they said you weren't there, I figured there must be something wrong." I stood to go. "I'll let you rest."

We said our goodbyes and when I was back in my car, I sat in the dark feeling numb. Irma had become a good friend in such a short time. Possibly the best friend I'd ever had. The thought that I might lose her so soon... I couldn't think about it. She'd make it through this scare. She had to. I wiped a tear from my cheek and started the engine.

Before putting the car in gear, I called Freddie, but the call went to voicemail. Considering it was Saturday evening and Freddie, unlike me, had a social life, she was probably on a date or out with friends. I didn't leave a message.

When I disconnected, I saw I had another message

from Kaslov—this time a text. *I need to speak with you as soon as possible.*

Why the vague message? I replied to the text and waited for an answer, but none came.

"This is probably a bad idea," I told myself, but part of me wanted something to distract my mind from Irma's condition. Backing the car out of Irma's driveway, I headed in the direction of The Amazing Kaslov's castle.

If I thought driving up the winding road to Kaslov's home seemed spooky in complete darkness, it was even creepier in the fading sunlight. Long shadows stretched over the road and small animals darted in front of my car, forcing me to slam on my brakes more than once.

Relieved to have arrived at the gates, I pulled to a stop. Before I turned the engine off, the gates opened, so I drove ahead and parked my car.

After crossing the little bridge, I found the front door ajar. As I pushed it open, it gave a long, slow creak. I took a deep breath and entered, calling out Kaslov's name.

The quiet interior unnerved me. The thick rugs muffled my footsteps as they would with anyone else who might sneak up on me. I crept through the hall ready for someone to jump out at me as if I were in a Halloween haunted house with teenagers waiting to prank me around every corner.

"Calm down," I told myself. "No one is out to get you."

The living room appeared welcoming with a

roaring fire. I was about to check for Martha in the kitchen when Thea entered through a door on the opposite side of the room. She wore a flowing, silk tunic and leggings. Her feet were bare.

"Oh, hello," she said, tilting her head to one side. "What are you doing here?"

Her reaction and question seemed odd since someone had seen my car and opened the gate. If it had been Kaslov, then where was he?

"I'm here to see your uncle," I explained. "He left me a message. I tried a number of times to call and text, but I couldn't get through or leave a message."

"Oh." She stared at me for several seconds while I waited, trying to be patient. "I can take you to him if you like."

"Yes, please."

She turned and exited the room through the same door she'd entered. I assumed this side of the castle led to the living quarters, but maybe there was a den or game room. There could even be a bowling alley in the basement for all I knew.

I followed her down a dark hallway. At the end, she opened a door and motioned for me to go ahead. As I reached the doorway, she flipped a switch and I found myself at the top of a flight of stairs. Maybe I'd been right about the bowling alley.

"I'll take that," she said, grabbing my purse and giving me a shove. She slammed the door behind me, and I stumbled, reaching out for the wall to steady myself and avoid falling down the stairs. Stunned, I swung around, trying to figure out what had just happened. I tried the handle, but it didn't turn.

Banging on the door, I called out, "Thea! Let me out."

I put my ear to the door but heard nothing on the other side. I banged again, my hope fading as the futility of my efforts began to sink in.

Thea had locked me in the basement. But why?

CHAPTER 14

*S*truggling to grasp what had just happened, I stood on the top stair for what felt like forever. At least she'd left the light on, but the single bulb hanging by the door didn't do much to illuminate the basement. Wondering what awaited me below, but not sure I wanted to know, I forced myself to take the first step.

I reached for the rail but pulled back when my hand touched a thick, sticky layer of dust. As I carefully made my way to the bottom of the stairs, I squinted into the near darkness of the small room with its low ceiling. Shapes lurked in the dim light, with boxes shoved against one wall and a few scattered pieces of furniture. I imagined the sound of rats scurrying along the edges of the walls and I shivered. Besides the chilling sound, it was even colder down here than in the main house. I rubbed my arms in a futile effort to warm myself.

A glimmer of hope flickered as I felt in my pocket.

My phone. That silly girl hadn't thought to take it from me. I pulled it out and dialed 9-1-1.

Nothing happened. The non-existent bars at the top of the screen told me why. The thick stone walls meant zero cell phone reception down here. I checked the battery, relieved to see it registered nearly a hundred percent. At least I had my flashlight app. After shining the light into the corners of the room and convincing myself there weren't any rats to worry about, I reluctantly turned my phone off to conserve power.

After pacing the floor for several minutes, I turned the phone back on and found a chair which I uprighted to give me somewhere to sit other than on the filthy floor. I dusted it off with my sleeve. Before turning my phone off again, I shined the light around the room again and nearly jumped when I saw a figure. Theadora's ghost watched me from the shadows.

"Oh, it's you." I wasn't in the mood to go around and around with her. "While you were telling me your brother was in danger, you might have also told me to watch out for your daughter."

She took a few steps toward me. "Why did you come back?"

"I had a message from Kaslov." Had the message really been from him? If he'd wanted to see me, then where was he?

"What message would he give you?" Theadora asked.

I closed my eyes and tried to remember. "Something about a secret he wanted to divulge before he died."

Theadora took a step closer. "But why you?" She laughed, an eerie, hollow sound. "He barely knows you."

"Oh." The realization came a little late. Thea had faked the call to get me here. But how had she done it? "The recording equipment in Kaslov's office. Thea must have fast-forwarded until she found just the message—something vague yet enticing. Your daughter is a clever young lady. Although, she did a very good job convincing everyone otherwise."

Theadora sighed and reached out to touch the stone wall. "This house has become a prison."

I stood and brushed myself off. "I'd certainly agree that the basement has become my prison. You realize your daughter locked me down here. Any idea what she has planned for me?"

Theadora didn't answer.

"That's okay. I have a pretty good idea." I began to fit the pieces together. "Thea killed Orson, didn't she?" I could see in my mind's eye the two young women talking to Mr. Featherman at my event. The dark-haired one had seemed familiar. Without her hair pulled back and the dark red lipstick, I hadn't recognized her at the time. She'd been playing two parts—a modern young woman at my event, cheerful and bubbly, and the morose recluse trapped in a castle. But which one was real?

"He humiliated her," Theadora said as if that were a perfectly good reason to kill someone.

"Do you mean Kaslov? Or Orson?"

Theadora didn't answer, just floated a few inches above the floor, glowing slightly in the darkness.

"Doesn't much matter now," I said. "Once you've stepped over that line once, the second time is easier." My suspicion grew into certainty that Thea intended for me to die down here.

"You shouldn't have come back," Theadora said. "I can't help you."

"And I can't help Kaslov. Not from the basement. Is he next?" I walked up to the ghost and jabbed a finger at her. No reaction. She seemed more like the memory of a ghost than a real spirit with thoughts and feelings. "Don't you care about your brother?"

She gazed at me with sad eyes. "There's nothing I can do."

"Why are you even here?" I asked.

"I—" She hesitated. "I'm not sure. I know this is not where I belong, but he won't let me go."

As I watched her, she faded away until she was nothing more than a wisp.

The basement might as well have been a dungeon with its stone walls and floors. All it lacked was chains bolted to the walls. I'd been in homes from the eighteenth and nineteenth centuries where the basement had originally been used for cooking and cleaning, but even though this place looked like an ancient castle on the surface, it had a modern kitchen and all the other amenities on the first floor.

I shone the light higher on the wall, and it flashed as it hit a metal surface—a square silver vent or opening of some sort. As I got closer, I realized the builders must have put in a laundry chute. Pulling the chair over to it, I stepped up and focused my phone's light into the interior. It rose at a 45-degree angle for about six feet then curved upward. There was no way to know where the other end of the tunnel emerged, and for all I knew it had been nailed shut. But it appeared to be my only chance to escape.

I held on and attempted to pull myself up, my feet scrambling on the cement wall for a non-existent foothold. It had been a few decades since I'd even attempted a pull up. I couldn't do one in my teens, so what made me think I could now?

Nevertheless, I tried again, my muscles screaming in pain. What I needed was a ladder, but I would have noticed one during my earlier search.

I turned my phone off and sat on the chair in the near darkness as the seriousness of my predicament sank in.

As I felt despair threaten to take over my thoughts, I could almost hear Irma's voice. "Are you afraid of dying?"

Was this it? Was this how my life would come to an end? Alone?

Then I recalled Freddie telling me, "Try and stay out of trouble, will you?" Would I even get to see her again? I'd do anything to hear her scold me for not listening to her.

Another memory. Jennifer saying, "If I can't have my mom around, I'm happy I have you." Jennifer was the closest I'd ever come to having a daughter.

They might not be with me in this dark basement,

but I wasn't alone. I had a family for the first time in my life. Not a family bound by blood but by kindness and loyalty and love.

"Okay, you guys," I said, pretending I was at my kitchen island with my three friends discussing our latest predicament. "How do I get out of this mess?"

"Use your brains," I imagined Irma saying.

"Think it through," came Freddie's voice.

I could almost see Jennifer smiling at me, innocent and wise. "I think there's a table over there. You could put the chair on top of it."

I spun around. Under the clutter and nearly hidden in shadow, I could make out the four legs of a table sticking up. I hurried over and moved a chair, two boxes, and a lamp from on top of it and turned the table over. Dragging it over to the chute, it screeched along the floor, but I doubted the sound would reach Thea or anyone else in the building.

With the table in position, I lifted the chair on top and climbed on the table. It wobbled back and forth, so I got down and moved it around until I found a more level spot. I positioned the chair just under the chute, the back of the chair even with the bottom.

Taking a deep breath, I climbed on the chair and stuck my head inside the chute and then the rest of my body. Pressing my arms and legs against the sides to keep me from sliding back down, I inched my way up.

I soon found myself able to look up into the vertical portion of the chute where light appeared to be coming through a crevice or gap. "Thank you," I murmured, still not knowing if I was any closer to safety.

Remembering my phone, I turned it back on, but it still showed no bars. Darned stone castle walls. I slowly pushed myself up to a kneeling position where I could look through the gap in what must be a door to the chute.

"Please don't let it be boarded up."

As I felt around with my fingers, tracing the outside, I heard voices. My heart leaped in my chest when I heard Martha's voice.

"You didn't eat your dinner," she said.

Thea's voice responded. "I'm not hungry."

I gasped in spite of myself, but luckily no one heard me. Not sure what else to do, I stayed put and listened to their conversation, waiting for Martha to be alone and hoping it wouldn't be long.

"Have you been snacking again?" Martha asked. "You have. You've been a naughty girl."

Martha, you have no idea.

"Just one piece of cake, please Martha?" Thea whined like an eight-year-old child.

Martha gave a dramatic sigh, then said, "Oh fine. Just one."

I waited for several long minutes until the two women said goodnight. Thea's footsteps faded as she left the room, and I held my breath listening for her return. Martha hummed as she put dishes in the dishwasher, then wiped her hands on a dishtowel. I gave the wooden cover blocking the opening a tentative push, but it didn't budge.

If I wanted Martha's help, I needed to act now before she left the kitchen. Not wanting to spend the night in a laundry chute, I called out softly, "Martha." When she didn't respond, I spoke a little louder. "Martha, it's April."

Her humming stopped and her eyes widened. She turned slowly. "What sort of game are you playing with me, Thea."

I called again. "It's not Thea, it's April. I'm in the laundry chute." I tapped on the cover.

She spun around seeking the sound of my voice and tapping, but she might not have even realized there was a laundry chute.

"Right ahead of you, near the floor," I said as loud as I dared. "I'm guessing it has some kind of a door over it." I tapped again to help her find me.

A moment later, the cover flung open, and light shone in.

Martha reached for my hand. "What the blazes are you doing in there?"

"Keep your voice down, please." I wasn't ready to feel safe with Thea somewhere in the building. "Thea locked me in the basement."

Between her pulling and my squirming, we managed to get me out. I brushed the dust off and gratefully collapsed into the chair she pushed toward me. Without my purse and car keys, I had no way to drive myself home. Another look at my phone showed I still had no reception.

"I need to make a call," I said. "Thea took my purse and my keys, and I'd like to have someone pick me up. Do you have a phone?"

"Who do you want to call?" she asked.

If I could get some privacy, I'd call Sheriff Fontana so he could come and arrest Thea. Not knowing how well that would go over, I said, "Freddie." When I got a blank look, I clarified, "Dr. Severs."

"I'll make the call from my room upstairs. Let me put the kettle on first." She filled the teakettle and put it on the stove. "Did you say Thea locked you in the basement?" When I nodded, she asked, "Why would she do that?"

"You'll have to ask her." I waited for her to say or do something, but she seemed to be making up her mind about something. "Can you make that call? I'd really like to go home."

"Yes, of course." She hurried out of the room, leaving me feeling vulnerable. What if Thea came back? I needed a weapon, so I opened several kitchen drawers until I found a steak knife. It might be rude to sit in someone's kitchen with a knife in my hand, but I'd gone beyond worrying about etiquette.

The kettle began to boil, and Martha reappeared and turned the fire off. "I called Freddie and she's on her way. I assume you like tea since you run a tearoom." She gave me a kind smile. "I hope chamomile tea is okay, that's all I have in the house right now." She poured two cups of tea and set one of them in front of me. "Sugar?"

"No, thank you," I said, grateful my ordeal would soon be over. I held the cup up to my mouth and breathed in the steam before taking a sip. I loved chamomile tea's honey-like sweetness without any sweetener.

"I'm so sorry about Thea. Sometimes I don't know what to do with her."

I said nothing. The girl belonged in jail, and that's where she'd be going as soon as Freddie took me to the police station.

"Young girls can do crazy things when they fall in love. You remember, don't you?" She didn't wait for me to answer. "I do. And when Orson told her he was leaving and he didn't want to be with her, she was devastated. Heartbroken."

I sipped the warm tea and listened to Martha's lilting voice, feeling calmer by the moment.

"Chamomile is so soothing, isn't it?" Martha said as she slid the knife away from me. "So, so soothing." Her hypnotic words washed over me. Everything would be okay.

My eyelids grew heavy. Something had gone wrong, terribly wrong, but I couldn't fight the drowsiness. "What time is it? It must be late."

"It's too late for you," Martha said.

CHAPTER 15

J groaned as I woke up on a stone floor, stiff and sore. "Not again." How could I be so stupid as to get myself thrown in the basement twice in one night? At least it wasn't as dark this time, and I had a blanket covering me.

My bleary eyes struggled to focus. The glow of early morning light filtered through narrow, grimy-looking windows. *Morning light?* My groggy mind struggled to figure out how I went from the kitchen having a cup of tea with Martha to spending the night on a hard, stone floor.

The tea. Those must have been some powerful sleeping pills or tranquilizers Martha had slipped into the tea.

With some effort, I rolled over and got on my hands and knees then crawled to the edge of the small round room. Using the wall to pull myself up, I leaned over the stone windowsill and gasped at the sight.

I had to be fifty feet or more above ground level. The tower, for that must have been what I was trapped in, overlooked the front of the castle. Below, I spied the footbridge and farther out, the gate at the end of the driveway.

But where was my car? Thea or Martha must have moved it and hidden it somewhere. How much was Martha involved with Thea's activities? Had she helped her kill Orson? I found the thought chilling, but I imagined Thea might have needed help sneaking out of the castle and finding her way to my tearoom.

Or maybe Martha was covering for Thea after the fact—protecting her as she grew from a troubled child into a troubled young woman out of a sense of misplaced loyalty.

Staring out the window, my hopes faded once again. If anyone thought to come looking for me and didn't find my car on the property, they'd never think to look for me within the castle walls.

To the north, I spotted the lighthouse and farther off my little town of Serenity Cove. Did my friends even know I was missing? They'd be waking up soon, getting ready for their days. Why hadn't I told someone I was coming to the castle yesterday? No one had any reason to look for me here.

My heart sank, and I turned away from the window, sliding down the wall until I was sitting on the cold, hard floor. The stone wall pressed into my back. Now what?

The small room had few furnishings. It had probably been designed to look impressive from the outside rather than being meant for a specific use. A child-sized vanity sat against one wall covered in dust. Using the window ledge, I pulled myself to standing. The druggy feeling had nearly worn off and my legs felt steadier. I walked over to the little vanity, pulling open the little drawers but finding nothing of any use for me in my predicament—a small doll, a handheld mirror and matching brush, and other things a young girl might like.

Thea must have spent time up here when she was a little girl. If I'd had such a place to play when I'd been young, I might never have come down, insisting that I move into the tower full time. But Thea had been trapped in this castle since she was a baby when her uncle had retreated from the world. One person's fairy tale can be another's horror story. What I needed was a length of rope or Rapunzel's long locks, so I could climb down from my tower for a happy ending.

Just to be thorough, I tried the door. Of course, it was locked. Even if I knew how to pick locks, I had no tools for the job. Or did I? I went back to the vanity and found a few hairpins in one of the drawers.

Taking some over to the door, I knelt on the hard floor and inserted one end of a hairpin into the lock. Surely, I remembered something from all the mysteries and thrillers I'd watched on TV. The opening was called the barrel and the pins were the little cylinders that had to be pushed out of the way. I fiddled with the hairpin getting nowhere until I couldn't ignore the pain coming from my knees and stood. I needed something to put on the floor to cushion it, but nothing in the room fit the bill.

A few other toys littered the floor, and I examined each briefly before returning to the window which I scrutinized. A rope would do me no good even if I had one. The thick glass pane had no opening, its only purpose was to allow light in.

Returning to the vanity, I found the heaviest item— the hairbrush—and took it back to the window. I slammed it against the glass, again and again, harder each time until the hairbrush broke in half. The glass hadn't even cracked.

How many times could I lose hope before I gave up completely? I shook off the idea just as another thought came to mind. Martha and Thea had left me no food or water, and that could only mean one thing. They'd left me here to die.

I leaned against the side of the window, watching the grounds for signs of life. Occasionally, a movement would catch my eye and I'd see a squirrel scurry up a tree or a bird swoop onto the lawn. Watching a few robins peck at the ground looking for worms, I almost forgot my predicament. I recognized them by their rust-red breast as they hopped and pecked at the grass.

I wished with all my heart I could talk to my friends, even if just one more time. And my brother and I hadn't been on good terms—it seemed a shame we might never have the chance to heal our relationship.

The sun came up over the trees and sunbeams lit the scene reminding me of a religious painting. I guessed it to be around eight in the morning. How long before Jennifer would knock on my door at home? She would call Irma or Freddie to find out if they knew where I was. But no one knew.

Another movement caught my attention. The gate opened and hope surged through my veins as Irma's 1985 Cadillac Eldorado drove through, parking right where I'd parked the day before. She and Freddie got out of the car and walked toward the footbridge.

I yelled as loud as I could, but no one even looked up. I picked up the broken hairbrush from the floor where I'd dropped it and banged it on the window as they walked toward the castle doors.

Hope faded as I imagined them walking through the castle hallway. Were they talking to Kaslov? Was Thea there?

Rushing to the door, I screamed and banged my fists against the thick wood making as much noise as I possibly could. Then I stopped and pressed my ear to the door. I couldn't hear a single noise on the other side, which probably meant they couldn't hear me either.

They'd talk to Kaslov who'd tell them I wasn't here, and then they'd leave and never come back. They'd wonder whatever happened to me, maybe organizing a search party to scour the woods. Days would go by, then weeks and months. Eventually, people would ask, "Do you remember that woman who disappeared one day? They never found out what happened to her."

After I passed, would I be a ghost? I could find someone to haunt or spend my eternity with Chef

Emile if I could figure out how to get my ghost-self home. Would I be able to walk right through the heavy wooden door? Maybe I'd float right through the castle walls and fly home.

Or maybe I'd be stuck here spending eternity with Theadora listening to her talk in circles.

CHAPTER 16

The thought of eternity with Theadora woke me from my dark reverie. "I have to get myself out of here now."

A sunbeam shone through the window as if it were a message from the heavens. I took one more look around the room. Would it work?

I threw open the drawers of the vanity, grabbed the hand mirror, and returned to the window. It wasn't long until Irma and Freddie emerged and walked toward their car. I held the mirror up to reflect the sun's light. Aiming the light at Irma's face, I flicked it—three fast, three slow, and another three fast.

She stopped, and I imagined the quizzical look on her face although I couldn't see her expression from so far away. I held up the mirror to send the SOS signal again just as a cloud floated in front of the sun.

"No!" Could I possibly be so close and fail?

I said a silent prayer and held up the mirror. The

cloud floated past, and I flashed the signal again. Irma grabbed Freddie's arm and pointed up at the tower.

Tears ran down my cheeks.

Irma and Freddie disappeared from view as they entered the castle again. I would soon be saved, and I did my best not to crumple in a sobbing heap. Instead, I banged on the door and yelled, "Help! I'm in here!"

Footsteps came up the steps and the door flung open, nearly knocking me over. Thea's eyes flashed with anger.

"Help!" I called as loudly as I could before she slammed the door behind her. I looked for something to hide behind, to protect me as I backed away from her. In desperation, I called out to the ghost who'd been nothing but a nuisance so far. "Theadora, please help me."

Thea slapped me hard, knocking me against the wall. "No one calls me that. Especially not you."

"I'm talking to your mother. Her ghost is here, with us, right now." I was lying, but she didn't know that. I had no idea if Theadora could appear up here in this tower.

Thea pulled a pocketknife from her coat pocket, slid the blade open, and stepped closer. "Shut up."

"After she died, she never left you. She watched your nanny brushing your hair when you were a little girl." I held up the broken hairbrush. "All the time, she wished she could be the one doing it."

She lunged for the hairbrush, and I jerked it away as I reached out one leg to trip her. The knife flew out of her hand as she fell, and we both scrambled for the weapon. I grabbed it first, but she picked up the hair-brush which I'd dropped in the scuffle and swung it wildly at me, knocking the knife out of my hand.

Theadora's ghost shimmered into view, but I didn't expect her to protect me from her daughter.

"Did Orson promise to take you away from all this?" I asked. "From this prison of your uncle's?"

"Hah!" she scoffed. "He said he would get rid of my uncle, and then all this would be ours. We would live here together happily ever after." Her lips pulled back in a snarl. "Instead, he planned to betray both of us. I overheard Orson demanding money from my uncle, and that's when I knew I'd have to do it myself."

"My poor sweet girl." Theadora's ghost spoke softly, then turned to me. "I used to watch Wendy brush Thea's hair in this room. She was like a mother to my dear child. How did you know?"

"Wendy?" I repeated as I inched away from Thea.

Thea's eyes widened. "How do you know about Wendy?"

The ghost sighed. "My brother sent her away. He thought they were getting too close."

I repeated what Theadora had said. "Just when you began to feel like you were loved and cared for, he fired her. How many others were there? How many times did he break your heart just to keep you under his control?"

Thea's mouth opened but no words came out, just a low moan as tears streamed down her face. She ignored the banging on the door and sunk to the floor in a heap as if all her will to fight had left her.

The door swung open and Kaslov stood in the doorway. When I saw Irma and Freddie behind him, I nearly collapsed with relief.

Kaslov hurried to Thea and crouched next to her. He gave me an accusing look. "What did you do to her?"

Thea clutched the lapels of his jacket. "You told me Wendy was tired of me. That I was too much trouble."

Irma hurried to my side while Freddie called the sheriff. Irma began asking questions, but I held up a hand—I wanted to hear what Thea and Kaslov said.

"Who are you talking about?" Kaslov asked Thea.

"My nanny. She—" Thea pointed at me. "She said you sent them away."

"Nonsense," Kaslov stood and put his hands on his hips. "What lies are you telling my niece? Can't you see she's disturbed?" He reached out a hand to help Thea to her feet.

Thea's eyes darted wildly around the room, and she grabbed something from the floor as Kaslov took her in his arms.

He stroked her back as he murmured, "We'll get you the very best help available."

"Yeah, right," I said. "After she stands trial for the murder of Orson Jennings."

As Thea reached her arm around Kaslov, a flash of light reflected off the knife I'd knocked out of her hand earlier. She held it pointing at his back, ready to plunge it into him.

Kaslov, watch out!" I grabbed Thea's arm just above the wrist and held on with all my might, doing my best to prevent her from stabbing him just as she must have done with Orson.

Kaslov managed to squirm out of her grasp, and I shook the weapon from her hand, letting it fall on the ground. This time, I picked it up to make sure Thea wouldn't get another chance to hurt anyone.

"Why, Thea?" Kaslov asked, staring at her angry face. "Why?"

"I hate you." She spat on his shoes and turned toward the door as if she planned to walk away.

Freddie slammed the door shut and stood in front of it. "You're not going anywhere. Not until Sheriff Fontana arrives."

I tugged on Freddie's arm. "Where's Martha?"

"Martha?" Freddie raised her eyebrows. "The cook?"

"She drugged me and helped Thea lock me in the tower. She could be getting away as we speak."

Freddie got back on the phone and gave the sheriff the additional information.

Soon, sirens wailed in the distance, becoming louder as they approached, and Irma hurried downstairs to direct the officers to the tower. I watched through the tower window as two cruisers sped through the gates. One of the cars parked across the drive blocking anyone from exiting. Sheriff Fontana jumped out of the other car and ran to the door followed closely by two deputies.

The sheriff and one of his deputies burst into the room and quickly handcuffed Thea. The deputy took her to the car as the sheriff conferred with Freddie.

"You need to find Martha and arrest her too," I said.

"Dr. Severs told me everything when she called," he said. "My other deputy is searching the house for her now. Are you all right? I wanted to send an ambulance, but Dr. Severs said she'd checked you out."

"Yes, I'm fine," I said. "Or at least I will be when I'm safe back at home."

He patted me on my shoulder. "You can wait downstairs if you'd prefer."

"I'll wait outside in front of the castle if that's okay. I'd rather not spend another minute inside these walls.

Half an hour later, after Thea and Martha were carted off to jail and Victor Kaslov had been taken in for questioning, Sheriff Fontana pulled me aside.

"Are you sure you're all right?" His voice, gentle and full of concern, caught me off guard. "I wish you had let me call an ambulance."

"My doctor is right over there." I gestured to Freddie who waited with Irma by the car. "She'll keep an eye on me. I guarantee it."

"Okay," he said reluctantly. "I'm going to need a complete statement from you, but that can wait until tomorrow. Will you be able to come by the station or would you like me to come to your place?"

I smiled for the first time that day. "The sheriff makes house calls?"

He returned my smile. "Only for you."

"That would be nice."

My gaze drifted to his hand where I spotted a wedding ring. He was married. Why was I surprised? Or a better question, why was I disappointed?

"See you tomorrow, Sheriff." I gave him a little wave as I headed for Irma's car.

"Straight home?" Freddie asked. "Or do you need to stop anywhere first?"

"Home," I said. "I've got a bottle of champagne in the fridge and we're going to celebrate the two of you rescuing me from the castle tower. By the way, what made you come here looking for me?"

"Get in the car, and we'll tell you all about it," Irma said. "Freddie can drive. I'm too worked up."

Irma insisted I take the front seat next to Freddie, and on the drive home, she leaned forward and told me how when Jennifer went to my room and saw my bed hadn't been slept in, she panicked.

"Jennifer called me," Freddie said, "and I called Irma. When she said you'd stopped by yesterday evening, and I told her I had a missed call from you, we both had a sinking feeling you'd gone back to the castle."

Irma tapped me on the shoulder to make sure she had my full attention. "Freddie had second thoughts when your car wasn't here. But I just had a feeling, and I wasn't about to give up until I knew what they were hiding. Turns out, they were hiding you."

"Thea and Martha were. I don't think Kaslov had any idea." I gave Irma a grateful smile. "Thank you for trusting your gut. I know it was stupid for me to go back by myself."

"Then why did you?" Freddie asked.

"I had a voice message and a text from Kaslov," I explained. "But it turns out neither one was from him. Thea must have gone through his Dictaphone tapes to find a cryptic message to record and send to me."

"People still use Dictaphones?" Irma asked.

"I think he was dictating his memoirs," I said. "And then he sent me the text saying he wanted to talk to me as soon as possible. Since I couldn't get either of you to go with me, I decided to go by myself. I had no idea I'd be putting myself in danger."

Irma eagerly asked, "How did you end up locked in the tower, anyway?"

I described my harrowing evening, starting with Thea throwing me in the basement and how I climbed out of the laundry chute.

Irma listened and nodded as if I'd accomplished something special. "I've never known anyone who's been thrown in a dungeon before."

"And then, when I thought the ordeal was over, Martha put something in my tea. They must have been some strong sleeping pills."

"Martha drugged you?" Irma's face turned bright red. "That— That—" She could hardly speak. "That witch! I hope they lock her up for a long, long time."

"I think we'll learn that Martha had a lot of influence on Thea and Kaslov," I said. "She was extremely possessive of both of them and didn't want to share them with anyone. She hated Orson. I won't be surprised if we learn that she helped plan his murder."

I leaned back in my seat letting the car rock me side to side as Freddie navigated the twisty road. Next thing I knew, Jennifer opened my car door and shook me awake.

"Are you okay?" she asked, her voice anxious.

"I'm fine," I assured her, but I allowed her to help me out of the car.

Freddie reached for one of my arms. "You're going straight to bed."

I pulled my arm back from her, not wanting to be treated like an invalid. "Not until I get something to eat. I'm starving. And not until we fit all the pieces together. I'll need you and Irma to help with that."

CHAPTER 17

Freddie wrapped me in a blanket and propped my feet up on an ottoman. She started a fire in the fireplace while Irma and Jennifer busied themselves in the kitchen.

I dug into a plate full of crispy bacon, over-medium eggs, and crunchy hash browns. Jennifer knew just the way I liked my breakfast. She made me a second cappuccino, but this one was decaf as ordered by Freddie.

"I totally freaked out when you weren't in your room this morning," Jennifer said, as she took a seat next to me on the sofa. "I could tell you hadn't slept in it."

"Good thing I don't make my bed first thing in the morning, or it might have been hours before you realized I'd gone missing."

"Good thing is right." Freddie sat in one of the armchairs.

"I still don't know what happened," Jennifer pouted. "Irma and Freddie wouldn't let me come with."

"I'll tell you everything but let's get Irma out here, so I don't have to repeat anything. I only gave her the short version in the car." The strain of the past two days began to catch up with me as the adrenaline slowly wore off.

Jennifer walked to the kitchen door and pushed it open. "I'll finish cleaning up later. Come on. April's going to tell me everything that happened."

Surrounded by my three friends, I explained about the cryptic voice message and urgent text I thought had come from Kaslov.

"Irma wasn't feeling well," I began, then turned to Irma. I didn't want to tell the others anything she wasn't ready to share. "Are you feeling better now?"

Irma dismissed my question with a wave of her arm. "We can talk about me later. So next you drove to the castle?"

"Yes, after Freddie didn't answer her phone. I had no reason to think I was in danger, so I drove up there to see what Kaslov wanted."

Everyone gasped when I told them how Thea had shoved me through the basement door then locked me in. I left out the part about seeing Theadora's ghost—I could tell Irma about that later when we were alone.

The women hung on my every word as I explained climbing out through the laundry chute. When I told them about Martha making me a cup of tea, Irma crossed her arms over her chest and scowled. I didn't know if she was angry at Martha or angry at herself for letting herself get fooled by the woman. Probably both.

I went on with the story, explaining how I'd woken up in the tower.

"Wait." Jennifer stopped me. "She drugged you? Then she helped Thea put you in the tower?"

"That's right." I left out how desperate I'd felt knowing that I might die in that tower. "I had no idea how I was going to get out of there, but when I saw these two show up..." My voice choked, and I took a sip of my drink while I composed myself.

Irma jumped in. "I'd told April how to tap SOS, and so she used a mirror to flash at me. At first, I thought it was just the sun reflecting off the windows, but when I realized there was a pattern, I looked to see where it came from. That's when I knew she was in the tower."

"I called 9–1–1," Freddie said, "then hurried after Irma who accosted Kaslov. She demanded he tell her how to get to the tower." She gave Irma a look of admiration. "You were very forceful."

"Our girl was trapped, and I had no idea what they'd done to her," Irma said, not hiding the pride she obviously felt.

"When we found April in the tower, I called Sheriff Fontana to fill him in. He was already on his way with reinforcements."

I told the rest from my point of view including the huge relief I felt when I saw Irma and Freddie in the doorway behind Kaslov.

"Thea tried to kill Kaslov?" Jennifer's mouth hung open.

"I think that's how she killed Orson," I explained. "That had me stumped—I figured the murderer had knocked him down and then stabbed him. But I think she wrapped her arms around him in an embrace, then plunged the knife into his back."

"Oh," Jennifer said with a grimace. "That's awful. How could someone have so much hate and anger in them?"

"We may never know," I said. "But I have a feeling Martha has been brainwashing her for a while. Maybe both her and Kaslov."

Irma spoke up. "I remember her talking Kaslov into teaching her how to hypnotize someone. That must be how she did it."

"Makes sense."

Jennifer still looked confused. "Are you saying Thea was here at the event? And no one recognized her?"

I STIFLED A YAWN.

Freddie stood. "Now it's off to bed for you."

I shook my head. "I want to stay right here. It's so comfy."

Freddie finally relented. "As long as you promise to rest. And get to bed early tonight. And make sure to call me if you feel woozy or have any other symptoms."

Irma gave me a kiss on the top of my head, Freddie squeezed my hand, and the two women left.

"I'll finish with the dishes." Jennifer headed for the kitchen.

"Can you leave the door open?" I asked. "I think I'll feel better if I can hear you."

She did as I asked, although I had another reason for wanting the door open. A few minutes later, Chef came into view.

He gave me a smile. "*Zut alors!* The scare you gave me, gave all of us." He watched me from the doorway, and just before I fell asleep, I heard him say, "I thought I had lost you, *ma chérie*. Sleep well."

CHAPTER 18

a sunbeam across my face woke me, and when I saw the time, I jumped out of bed. After the briefest of showers, I dressed and hurried downstairs where I found Jennifer in the kitchen. We opened in less than an hour.

"What do you mean we're closed today?" I asked Jennifer. "It's Sunday." I checked my phone to make sure I hadn't slept through to Monday. Nope, today was definitely Sunday. "I thought I'm the one who decides when we're open and when we're not. It's my tearoom, after all."

"Doctor's orders," Jennifer said.

As if on cue, Freddie entered through the back door. "How are you feeling today?"

"I'm fine." I might have whined when I said it. "Uninjured and unharmed. There's no reason I can't work today."

"You were drugged, trapped in a basement *and* a tower, and you were just rescued yesterday." Freddie gave me a skeptical look. "You're not the least bit trau-matized?"

"I'll make mochaccinos for both of you while you talk it out," Jennifer said.

I'd just taken a seat at the island when a crash made me scream and jump off my stool.

"Sorry," Jennifer said, surrounded by the pieces of a saucer that had slipped out of her hand. "I'll clean it up."

"A little jumpy?" Freddie asked. "Face it. You need a few days to recover. Take some time off and do some-thing fun or relaxing.

"Like what?" I'd worked all my life. I wasn't sure I knew how to relax. I could get a massage or a pedicure, but that wouldn't take up more than a couple of hours.

A knock on the back door sounded familiar, and I was pleased to see Mark join us. After greeting every-one, he pulled me aside.

"I heard you weren't going to open the tearoom today. I thought you might like to go for a ride up the coast. Maybe to Mendocino. Or we could head for San Francisco if you'd rather."

"A drive up the coast sounds wonderful," I admitted. "Give me a few minutes to grab some things and I'll meet you out front."

After grabbing my purse and jacket, I came back downstairs and said goodbye to Freddie and Jennifer, wondering which one of them had told Mark I'd be free that day, not that it mattered.

Chef Emile gave me a longing look, and I wondered if he'd be lonely with me gone all day. I didn't understand why. After all, as far as I knew he'd spent decades with no one he could talk to.

"What is it?" Freddie asked. "Are you feeling up to an outing?"

"Of course." I hurried to meet Mark outside.

One look at his work truck and I suggested we take my car. Mark agreed as long as I let him drive. As we headed out of town, we approached the turnoff for The Amazing Kaslov's castle.

"Can we make a little side trip?" I asked. When he gave me a questioning look, I added, "There's a road up ahead on your left. It won't take long."

Mark turned onto the winding road. "Isn't this the road to Kaslov's place?" When I nodded, he asked, "Are you sure you want to do this?"

"He's all alone," I said. "Besides, this time I have you with me."

Mark smiled. "I've always wanted to see the place. I heard it's pretty awesome." His smile faded and he glanced at me. "He might not want to see you, you know."

"I know." After all, I'd been responsible for putting his niece and his housekeeper in jail. He'd gone from having three people for company to none. I couldn't help but think he must be terribly lonely.

When we made the last curve and came upon the castle grounds, the gate stood open. Mark drove through and parked. Even the birds seemed subdued as they softly chirped and tweeted.

Mark tried to take in everything, saying "wow," so

many times I lost count. We crossed the little bridge to the front door.

Mark examined the dragon door knocker. "Cool."

"You may do the honors," I said, gesturing to the door.

He lifted the dragon and let it fall, then repeated the action, but no one came to the door.

"Try again," I suggested.

He thumped the knocker a few more times and we waited for several minutes but no one arrived to greet us. Eventually, I had to admit that either Kaslov wasn't home, or he didn't want visitors.

I sighed. "I'll come back another time."

Theadora appeared in front of me. "Don't go."

Mark sensed my hesitation. "What is it?"

I paused, not sure what I wanted to say, but getting tired of lying to people. "This isn't how I planned to tell you." I liked Mark and I had a feeling he liked me. If we were going to get closer, I couldn't keep things from him. But I'd wanted more time to figure out just how to tell him I could see ghosts. I had no idea how he would take the news.

"Tell me what?" he asked. "I don't like the look on your face. It's something bad, isn't it?"

With a big sigh, I made my decision. "I can see ghosts."

He laughed. "What are you talking about? Oh, I get it. You take me to the spooky castle and then tell me it's haunted. If you want me to hold your hand, you just have to ask."

He reached for my hand, but I kept my arms by my

side. "Never mind." I looked at Theadora. "We're leaving."

Theadora's eyes pleaded with me. "Please go talk with him."

Why had I asked Mark to drive up here? I wanted to see Kaslov, to find out if I could help him. I walked back to the front door.

"I thought we were leaving," Mark said, obviously confused by my actions.

I tried the handle and pushed the door open. I glanced back at Mark raising my eyebrows, and when he shrugged in response, I entered. After a moment, he followed.

I led him down the hall and into the living area, the only sounds coming from our muffled footsteps on the carpet.

"Kaslov?" I called out but got no answer.

Mark said "wow" a few more times as he examined the room, moving from the fireplace to the leaded glass windows and back to me. "Where is everyone?" he asked. "He must have staff, right?"

"He did before his niece, Thea, killed his butler and she and the cook locked me in the tower."

"Wow."

Not expecting to find anyone there, I peeked into the kitchen and then led Mark to Kaslov's office.

Mark whispered, "This place has a lot of halls, doesn't it?"

I knocked on the office door and a voice replied, "Come in if you must." I stepped into the room, Mark hesitating in the doorway.

Kaslov stopped in the middle of emptying the contents of one of the bookcases into a box and straightened up. "Oh, it's you. What do you want?"

Theadora stood near the window, anxiously clutching her hands. She gave me a pleading look. What did she expect me to do or say?

"I wanted to see how you are," I said. "You're moving?"

His eyes swept around the room before returning to me. "I can't stay here. There are too many ghosts."

"You know about Theadora?" Too late, I realized he wasn't being literal. "Oh, you mean ghosts as in memories."

"That's the second time you mentioned Theadora. I said no one calls Thea that, and you said... what did you say?"

"I think I said, 'I wasn't talking about Thea,' if I recall correctly." I waited for a reaction, but Kaslov seemed beaten and unable or unwilling to argue with me. "She's in this room right now. Your sister, I mean."

After regarding me with an expression I couldn't decipher, he shuffled to his desk and sank into his chair. "I've always felt her presence. She wants to punish me. I've made so many mistakes, but I swear I only wanted to keep Thea safe. It's all my fault Theadora died."

"He's not to blame," Theadora said. "I heard the midwife talking. My death was sudden and unexpected, and the best hospital or doctor couldn't have saved me."

I took a seat on the other side of the desk. "She

doesn't blame you. Even if she'd been in a hospital, they couldn't have saved her." I watched him take in my words. "She's here now because she's worried about you."

"But what about what happened with Thea? Everyone knows she turned out the way she did because I was so overprotective."

I shook my head. "I don't think that's what happened. Irma told me that you taught some of your skills to Martha. We think she used some of those skills to influence your niece. And you."

His eyebrows drew together. "But how?"

"We may never know," I admitted. "Where will you go?"

He shook his head slowly. "Far, far away. Somewhere no one has heard of The Amazing Kaslov. My home, this castle, will be put up for sale." He paused. "But Theadora..."

"I think Theadora has stayed here because you couldn't let go of her, of her memory and your guilt. I'll leave you two alone. I know you can't see or hear her but let her know you'll be okay. Let go."

He nodded, and I turned to go. Mark still stood in the doorway looking dumbstruck.

"Come on," I said, and he followed me outside and stayed behind me as I walked over the little bridge and over to my car. I took one last long look at the fairy-tale castle and hoped that whoever moved in next would have a happier ending to their story.

CHAPTER 19

$\mathcal{M}$ark said little as we drove, and after about an hour he pulled the car over alongside a remote beach and shifted into park.

He turned in his seat to face me. "You see ghosts."

"Yes," I said. "It only started when I came to town. At first, I thought it was just the one ghost, but now I've seen two more. I can't explain it."

His gaze shifted and he stared out the windshield at the ocean waves. "I'm not sure I can do this, April."

"Do what? Go for a drive?"

He sighed. "It kind of freaks me out." He glanced at me. "I really like you. I thought maybe, I don't know. I thought we might end up together. I think I've felt that way since I first met you."

My stomach gave a little twist. "I think I felt that way too. But now?"

He shook his head. "Now I don't know."

"Because it kind of freaks you out?" I asked.

"Yeah."

I'd been given many reasons why someone didn't want to be in a relationship with me, but this was a whole new experience for me. Part of me thought that if he cared about me the way he claimed, it wouldn't matter. But that wasn't being fair to him.

"We can still be friends, right?" I asked.

He grimaced, but it was so fast I might have been mistaken. He forced himself to smile. "Sure."

The drive home felt like it lasted forever, and when we got out of the car, I said a quick goodbye and hurried up the steps.

Jennifer greeted me with, "What are you doing back so soon?"

I headed for the stairs, planning to go straight to my room. "I don't want to talk about it right now." As I fought back tears, something stopped me from going upstairs. Instead, I headed for the kitchen.

As the door swung closed behind me, I whispered, "Chef?" There was no answer. What would I do if Chef left me? I'd gone my whole life without him, but now I couldn't imagine my future without the cranky ghost. "Chef, where are you?" I heard the quaver in my voice.

Chef shimmered into view, a glass of wine in his hand and a hint of a smile on his handsome face.

Relief washed over me. "You're here."

"I have told you many times, *ma chérie*," he said with a twinkle in his eye. "I am always here."

∽

IF YOU'D LIKE to learn what happens next, preorder Tea is for Traitor, the next Haunted Tearoom Cozy Mystery.

SIGN up for updates at https://karensuewalker.com and see all my books at https://karensuewalker.com/books.

AND READ ON FOR RECIPES!

RECIPES

OPEN-FACED RADISH SANDWICHES

Yield: 6 to 8 servings

INGREDIENTS

- 1 French baguette
- 2 bunches of radishes
- Herbed butter

HERBED BUTTER INGREDIENTS

- ¼ pound unsalted butter, room temperature
- 1 ½ teaspoons minced scallions
- 1 ½ teaspoons minced fresh dill
- ½ teaspoon freshly squeezed lemon juice
- ½ teaspoon kosher or sea salt

- Pinch freshly ground pepper if desired

HERBED BUTTER INSTRUCTIONS

Combine all ingredients in a mixer at low speed or by hand until well mixed but not whipped.

ASSEMBLY INSTRUCTIONS

1. Slice baguette diagonally and toast lightly.
2. Wash and thinly slice radishes.
3. Butter toast with herbed butter, top with sliced radishes, and serve.

April's note: This is a simple, fresh appetizer and surprisingly elegant!

CRIME SCENE CAKE (AKA CHOCOLATE BEETROOT CAKE)

YIELD: 6-8 SERVINGS

INGREDIENTS

- 250 g beets (about 4 medium beets)
- 200 ml corn oil or other mild tasting oil
- 3 large eggs
- 1 tsp vanilla extract
- 180 g (about 1 ½ cups) flour
- 2 tsp baking powder
- 1 tsp baking soda
- 1 tsp salt
- 75 g cocoa powder (about ½ cup)
- 250 g sugar (about 1 cup)

INSTRUCTIONS

1. Scrub beets and boil for 30-40 minutes.
2. Preheat oven to 350° F (180° C).

3. Line one 8" cake pan with parchment/grease-proof paper.
4. Peel, chop, and puree beets in blender until smooth (should be 1 cup puree).
5. Add eggs to blender one at a time.
6. Add oil and vanilla extract to beet mixture and blend briefly until combined.
7. Mix dry ingredients in a medium to large bowl.
8. Add beet mixture to dry ingredients and fold in gently.
9. Pour into cake pan and bake for 50-60 minutes or until inserted skewer comes out clean.
10. Turn out onto cake rack to cool. Sift powdered sugar on top and serve.

April's note: The recipe listed metric measurements, so I've done my best to convert to U.S. volumes for those without a scale. But I highly recommend buying yourself a digital scale!

PARSNIP AND CARROT SOUP

Yield: 2 servings

INGREDIENTS

- 1-2 Tbsp cooking oil
- 1 onion chopped
- 1-2 chopped garlic cloves
- 2 carrots, roughly chopped
- 2 parsnips, roughly chopped
- 1 stock cube or 1-2 14-ounce cans broth
  (vegetable or chicken stock or broth will
  work)
- 1-2 cups water
- 1 Tbsp lightly chopped parsley
- 1 tsp thyme
- salt and pepper to taste
- ½ to 1 cup milk as desired

INSTRUCTIONS

1. Brown onion and garlic in oil in a medium to large saucepan.
2. Add root vegetables, stock cube and water (or broth), parsley, and thyme. Add enough water so vegetables are submerged and simmer over medium heat until tender.
3. Puree in a blender or with immersion blender.
4. Return to saucepan over low heat and add milk until desired color and consistency is achieved.
5. Heat through (don't boil) and serve.

SWEET POTATO BISCUITS

YIELD: ABOUT 24-30 BISCUITS

INGREDIENTS

- 2 ½ cups flour
- 2 Tbsp baking powder
- ¾ tsp salt
- ½ cup cold vegetable shortening or unsalted butter
- 1 egg, well beaten
- ¾ cup milk
- 1 ½ cups mashed sweet potatoes (allow to cool before using)

INSTRUCTIONS

1. Preheat oven to 400° F (200° C).
2. Sift first three ingredients together.
3. Cut in shortening or butter until mixture resembles coarse crumbs.

4. Combine egg, milk, and sweet potatoes, then add to first mixture.
5. Chill dough for several minutes.
6. Knead lightly on floured surface, then roll ½ inch thick.
7. Cut with floured cutter and place biscuits on greased baking sheet.
8. Brush with milk and bake at 400°F (200°C) for 15 minutes.
9. Remove from oven and serve warm.

CARAMEL CINNAMON MUFFINS

YIELD: ABOUT 18 MUFFINS

INGREDIENTS

- 3 Tbsp butter
- 2/3 cup firmly packed brown sugar
- 2 cups flour
- 3 tsp baking powder
- ½ tsp salt
- 1 tsp cinnamon
- 1 egg, well beaten
- 1 cup milk
- 2 Tbsp melted butter

INSTRUCTIONS

1. Grease muffin pans and place ½ tsp butter and 1 tsp brown sugar in each cup.
2. Sift flour, baking powder, salt, and cinnamon together.

3. Combine milk, melted butter, egg, and remaining brown sugar.
4. Add to dry ingredients, stirring only enough to dampen flour.
5. Fill prepared muffin pans ¾ full and bake at 425°F (220°C) for 20 minutes.

STORM WARNING

YIELD: ONE DRINK

INGREDIENTS

- 10 mL (2 teaspoons) lime juice
- 30 mL (2 Tablespoons) spiced rum
- 150 mL (5 ounces) ginger beer
- 1 lime wedge for garnish
- 1 piece of crystallized ginger for garnish
- Ice

INSTRUCTIONS

1. Add spiced rum, ginger beer, lime juice, and ice to a glass.
2. Stir, then garnish with a skewer with the lime wedge and crystallized ginger
3. Serve!

April's note: If you don't have ginger, just put the lime wedge on the edge of the glass—I won't tell!

9 781955 610094